CW01629687

Beth Lanc … our cocoa, Father.'

The m … n. Wycliffe apologize…

'I must…

Simon Lander asked: 'Are you staying overnight?'

'I'm booked in at the village pub.'

Lander looked disapproving. 'At the pub? You'll find it's pretty basic.'

'I expect I shall survive.'

Wycliffe let himself out by the white gate with a sense of relief, almost of having escaped. A certain tension was to be expected but in all his dealings with families he had rarely experienced such an awareness of separate individuals between whom there was no common ground, no accord; only suspicion and hostility. Grandfather, father, mother, and daughter were continuing to live together in the same house long after all but the most conventional bonds had disappeared. It was not what they had said or done, it was a matter of attitude, of atmosphere . . .

W.J. Burley lived near Newquay in Cornwall, and was a schoolmaster until he retired to concentrate on his writing. His many Wycliffe books include, most recently, *Wycliffe and the Guild of Nine*. He died in 2002.

By W.J. Burley

WYCLIFFE SERIES

Wycliffe and the Three Toed Pussy
Wycliffe and How To Kill a Cat
Wycliffe and the Guilt Edged Alibi
Wycliffe and Death in a Salubrious Place
Wycliffe and Death in Stanley Street
Wycliffe and the Pea Green Boat
Wycliffe and the School Bullies
Wycliffe and the Scapegoat
Wycliffe in Paul's Court
Wycliffe's Wild-Goose Chase
Wycliffe and the Beales
Wycliffe and the Four Jacks
Wycliffe and the Quiet Virgin
Wycliffe and the Winsor Blue
Wycliffe and the Tangled Web
Wycliffe and the Cycle of Death
Wycliffe and the Dead Flautist
Wycliffe and the Last Rites
Wycliffe and the Dunes Mystery
Wycliffe and the House of Fear
Wycliffe and the Redhead
Wycliffe and the Guild of Nine

HENRY PYM SERIES

A Taste of Power
Death in Willow Pattern

OTHER NOVELS

The Schoolmaster
The Sixth Day
Charles and Elizabeth
The House of Care

Wycliffe

AND THE DEAD FLAUTIST

W. J. Burley

AN ORION PAPERBACK

First published in Great Britain in 1991
by Victor Gollancz Ltd
First published in paperback in 1992
by Corgi Books
This paperback edition published in 2005
by Orion Books Ltd
Orion House, 5 Upper St Martin's Lane,
London WC2H 9EA

Copyright © W.J. Burley 2005

The right of W.J. Burley to be identified as the author of this work has been asserted by him in accordance with the Copyright, Designs and Patents Act 1988.

All rights reserved. No part of this publication may be reproduced, stored in a retrieval system, or transmitted, in any form or by any means, electronic, mechanical, photocopying, recording or otherwise, without the prior permission of the copyright owner.

A CIP catalogue record for this book
is available from the British Library.

Printed and bound in Great Britain by
Clays Ltd, St Ives plc

The Orion Publishing Group's policy is to use papers that are natural, renewable and recyclable products and made from wood grown in sustainable forests. The logging and manufacturing processes are expected to conform to the environmental regulations of the country of origin.

www.orionbooks.co.uk

The events described in this book take place on the River Fal, near Truro, in Cornwall. Many people will be able to identify the approximate locality but they will not find the Duloe Estate, nor will they find the Bottrells, the Landers, or the Biddicks, for all the people in this story are imaginary, and so are the events in which they become willingly, or unwillingly involved.

Chapter One

A Sunday in August, almost midnight; the night was soft and still, moonless but starlit. On a broad promontory between two creeks of the River Fal, the Duloe Estate spread out in a pattern of light and shade; the sweep of the park and the random patches of woodland disguised contours, creating here and there pools of deep shadow. Duloe House, home of the Bottrells, square and stark, commanded the landscape as it had done for two hundred years. Outbuildings formed two courtyards behind the house and, at some distance, nearer the upper creek, there was a second house, neither as old nor as large as Duloe, a building of low eaves, steep gables, and tall chimneys – Treave, home of the Landers. Inland from the estate, a half-mile from the river, a village of fifty or sixty houses, clustered and straggled about its church and pub.

There were two or three lighted windows in the village, an isolated cottage on the estate showed a single light, an upper window at Treave glowed plum-red through its velvet drape, but Duloe House was in total darkness. Everywhere there was stillness and it seemed there could be no living creature abroad. But in the shadow of a shrubbery, under the lighted window at Treave, Paul Bottrell, a boy of sixteen, waited.

He did not know how long he had been there and he had all but given up hope when he heard a faint sound, a sound repeated close at hand, a movement of the air, and a whispered: 'Hi!'

'I was afraid you wouldn't come.'

'Sh! That's mother's room and I don't think she's in bed yet.'

He felt her hand in his, warm and confident. They moved off, keeping to the grass border of the drive.

A few yards, and they turned off the drive along a footpath through the shrubbery; the shrubs gave place to trees and the trees made strange patterns against the sky. Although there was no moon outlines were clear.

'Listen!'

Someone was playing a flute, a melody, plaintive and melancholy. Paul put his arm around her. 'Jean!'

She said: 'Doesn't Tony ever go to bed?'

They could see the light from the cottage. The sound of the flute grew louder and the tune changed; the melancholy air gave place to the lifting rhythm of a reel which quickened the pulse. The light was in a downstairs room, the front door was shut, and a blind covered the window. On the blind the shadow of the flute player was enlarged and grotesque.

Paul said: 'He's a strange man.'

'Don't you like him?' Jean wanted definition.

Paul, always wary of committing himself, hesitated, then: 'I don't know; sometimes when he looks at me he makes me feel odd.'

They emerged from the woodland into the park. Duloe House brooded on its eminence, blind and silent. They walked, hand in hand down the slope to the river, through a belt of trees, and came upon a wharf largely overgrown by brambles and gorse. Beyond, the river ran smooth and luminous between shadowy banks.

Paul said: 'The skiff?'

'All right.'

On that other occasion, exactly a week ago, similar words had been spoken and already it was as though they were adhering to an established ritual. They followed a path through the undergrowth along the wharf and came to a boathouse. It rose in front of them, low to the eaves, but with a great expanse of roof. Paul opened a door in the side of the building and Jean followed him in. The house was open at one end to the river but it was eerie in the near darkness. Soft, liquid sounds came from movements of the water below the staging on which they stood.

The wet dock was occupied by a white launch which loomed large in the dim light and confined space. They passed around the bow of the launch to the other side of the dock where a cranky little river skiff was moored beside the launch. They got in, cast off, and Paul propelled the boat out of the house by working hand over hand along the staging. Once in the open river he unshipped the oars.

'Lower Creek?'

'No, let's do the same as last week.' Then they had followed the Upper Creek and almost reached the village.

'We shan't get far, the tide's too low.'

'Never mind.'

The little boat slid along, the water chuckling beneath the bow. Paul rowed cleanly, without splash. Now that they were on the water it seemed lighter and they could see each other clearly.

Paul said: 'I can't believe this.'

'What?'

'Well, all our lives we've lived next door to each other and, until I went away to school, we saw each other nearly every day . . . Even after that there were holidays . . . Now it's as though I've never known you.'

'And this holiday is nearly over.'

He stopped rowing. 'Don't, Jean!' He shipped the oars and came to sit beside her in the stern, leaving the boat to drift. She let him draw her to him and kiss her on the lips. He kissed her hair, her ears, and her neck and fondled her breasts.

Then there was a shot. It was not particularly loud; it sounded muffled, but it reverberated briefly between the banks.

Jean broke away. 'What was that?'

'A shot.'

'I know that, idiot! But who goes shooting in the middle of the night?'

'Somebody after a fox, or it could be poachers after old Roskilly's deer. They've tried it before.'

Jean got up and moved, cautiously, to the centre thwart. 'I'll row for a bit.'

'Are you angry with me?'

'Should I be?'

She gave the shore a wide berth and entered the creek, following the channel. Here the creek was broad but it narrowed quickly so that half a mile away, in the village, it was no more than a stream. The church tower rose out of the trees in silhouette against the night sky and the water was dark and shining. Once they were startled by a sudden quacking from the shore as something disturbed a family of roosting ducks.

Rounding a small promontory on their left they came in sight of an old cottage from which there had once been a ferry, now Treave property.

Paul said: 'There's a light in the cottage. Your father must be there again.'

The girl said nothing.

'Does he often spend the night there? I thought he only used it for his photography.'

'He sleeps there at weekends sometimes.' Her manner was distant, dismissive.

She continued rowing as the creek narrowed until

finally the keel ploughed into soft mud. It was of no consequence on a rising tide.

Jean said: 'Anyway, it's time I was getting back.'

'Already?'

Somehow the magic of the night had deserted them.

She back-paddled clear of the mud until the channel broadened and she was able to head the boat downstream. As they passed the cottage a light was still burning in an upper window but nothing was said.

They reached the boathouse in silence, berthed the skiff, and retraced their steps across the wharf. Paul put his arm around her. 'What's wrong, Jean?'

'Nothing. Don't be silly.'

They walked up through the park and as they entered the wood she said: 'Tony is still up.'

The way ahead seemed brightly lit and as they drew near the flute player's cottage they saw that the light came not only from the window but also through the open door.

Paul said: 'That seems odd. Perhaps we ought to find out if he's all right.'

'I don't want to be seen. He might tell my parents.'

'All right; you wait here.' The boy went ahead; she saw him standing in the doorway and she heard him call, softly: 'Tony? Are you there?' Then he went inside and a moment later she saw his shadow on the blind.

The door opened directly into the living-room. Paul knew the place well and everything looked as usual but there was a smell – acrid, and vaguely familiar, though he could not identify it. Then he rounded the draught screen and he could see the rest of the room.

Tony Miller was sitting in his usual chair by the window, his flute on the table at his elbow. He had a shotgun between his thighs, the butt resting on the floor, the muzzle pointed at his throat. Paul knew about shotguns but he had never before seen the consequence of a full charge entering a living creature at close range. The lower part of Tony's face had gone, leaving only a mess of blood and tissue. Blood had spattered the wall and the plastic covering of the table; even the gleaming flute was spotted and streaked with blood.

Paul felt faint. He turned away and steadied himself with one hand gripping the edge of the table.

Jean had heard nothing since he disappeared inside and it seemed a long time. The light, streaming across the clearing, intensified the shadows where it failed to reach. The silence was total and she began to feel uneasy. Then she heard soft footsteps, they sounded stealthy and seemed to come from somewhere close to the cottage. Peering against the light, she made out a vague figure standing by the corner of the building. It seemed that he (she was sure that it was a man) must have come round from the back. She had a momentary glimpse of the pale blur of his face then, immediately, he withdrew. Had he spotted her? She must have been easily visible in the stream of light from the cottage.

She decided to join Paul and ran across the clearing. He met her at the door and spoke in a horrified whisper. 'He's dead! He's been shot!'

'*Shot?*'

'I think he's killed himself.'

Chapter Two

The day before – Saturday – the Wycliffes had returned from a three-week holiday in the Dordogne. They had been there before – twice, and he had secretly entertained the notion that he might settle there on his retirement and take up fishing. There were difficulties: his French was not very good, he found the summers too hot, he had never fished in his life, and he did not particularly like Frenchmen. Added to that he guessed that if he broached the idea to Helen she would say: 'Over my dead body!'

As it was he had spent three weeks half-dazed by heat, sunshine, and white wine. He had vague recollections of delicious meals and convivial evenings at a restaurant just a few yards (metres) down the road from their cottage. (The cottage was rented from a countess who personally checked the cutlery, crockery, and linen, before they left.) He remembered the cathedral at Périgueux with its five great domes, the caves at les Eyzies, and a street scene in Sarlat where they were dress-rehearsing an outdoor performance of Henry V.

It was all very pleasant in a dreamlike way but secretly, towards the end, he missed the unpredictable showers, the smell of moist earth in the garden, even those murky days when everything drips. But as luck would have it they returned home to a heatwave, the garden was parched and within hours of their arrival Helen had produced an alarming list of plant casualties.

'I'll bet,' Wycliffe said, 'there's a hosepipe ban.'

On Monday morning he was on his way to the office, stuck in a queue for the ferry, breathing the usual cocktail of lethal gases from other people's exhaust. Oddly, when he got there, the sight of the police building, for all its naked ugliness, lifted his spirit. His parking space, labelled with his name and rank, and a welcoming grin from the desk sergeant, completed his home-coming.

He spent half an hour with the chief chatting about police and office politics, and an hour or so with his own deputy, John Scales, being briefed on progress or lack of it in cases on hand. Through the files he renewed old acquaintances and met new ones.

At half-past eleven Wycliffe had his office to himself, a chance to ease his way back into the burrow, but it did not last. Diane's voice came through on the intercom: 'Mr Kersey wants to see you.'

'Ask him to come in.'

Detective Inspector Doug Kersey, colleague of nearly twenty years.

Coming back after three weeks' absence can be like wearing new spectacles; one sees familiar faces with a keener perception. Wycliffe thought Kersey looked older. Certainly the grey hairs were taking over, spreading upwards from the temples; and his face, always deeply lined, now seemed furrowed. Wycliffe sighed.

'Good holiday, sir?'

'Fine! How are Joan and the girls?'

The civilities over, Kersey hooked up a chair and sat down. 'I reckon they've been saving this one for you. I've had Tom Reed on the line and he thinks he's got a homicide dressed up as suicide . . . Mind if I smoke?'

The question was rhetorical, but today there was a difference: Kersey came out with a pouch of tobacco, a little machine, and papers. 'I thought the chore of making 'em plus the lousy taste might put me off.'

'Where, and who?'

'The Duloe Estate, on the river, four or five miles south of Truro.'

'Isn't that the Bottrell place?'

Kersey referred to his notes. 'Let's get it right: Hugh Cuthbert Grylls Bottrell, Ninth Baron Bottrell.'

'Is it the noble lord himself?'

'No, the estate foreman: Anthony Charles Miller, bachelor, mid-thirties. He lives – lived – in a cottage on the estate. A girl, out dog-walking, found him. To be accurate, her dog did. He'd been shot with a 12-bore at very close range making a nasty mess of his face and neck.'

'So where does the notion of suicide come from?'

Wycliffe had to wait while Kersey concentrated on inserting a cigarette paper into his little machine.

'When he was found Miller was sitting in his chair—'

'He was indoors?'

'Yes. Didn't I say?'

'I wish you'd get that thing going then concentrate on what you're supposed to be telling me.'

Kersey grinned. 'Sorry! I expect I'll get better at it; I had an uncle who could roll these things with one hand. Anyway, Miller was in his living-room, sitting in his chair, the gun between his thighs, butt resting on the floor, muzzle pointing at his neck. There was a bit of string tied to the trigger – typical of a suicide with a long-barrelled shotgun. But Tom Reed is no fool and he says it's one for us.'

'I'll have a word with the chief.'

'Before you do there's something else you should know. The girl who found him is Simon Lander's daughter.'

'Lander, the lawyer?'

'And member of the Police Authority as ever was. The Landers are neighbours of the Bottrells. According to Reed, their house, Treave, was built on estate land. What's more, the Landers have been lawyers to the Bottrells since they wrote with a goose quill on parchment. Anyway, I gather Lander is already on Tom's back, convinced that Miller committed suicide and that Tom is stirring things unnecessarily.'

'You'd better contact Franks; we must have a path. report before the body is moved, and with a question between suicide and murder we shall need ballistics evidence. Get Melville down. As far as our people are concerned: scenes-of-crime there as soon as possible, Lucy Lane with a couple of DCs first thing in the morning and, if we're still in business, you can follow when you've off-loaded whatever you're on at the moment. Ask Truro to arrange accommodation – they can book me in at the village pub from tonight – if there is one and if they've got a room.'

It was one of his idiosyncracies to stay at places most likely to offer local contacts. In his lectures to cadets he was fond of saying: 'In any murder investigation if you shut yourself off from the locals you are working with one hand tied behind your back.'

Kersey said: 'If you start getting organized now, it will still be evening before you get there.'

'So what? The evenings are light and I shall have a chance to talk to Reed on the ground.'

He did not say that a day or two by the Fal might help dispel any lingering withdrawal symptoms from the Dordogne.

Kersey fingered fragments of tobacco from his lips and grinned. 'As I said, perhaps they laid this one on as a welcome home.'

'I'm going out to lunch – coming?'

'No, I promised Joan . . .'

He went to his usual restaurant, run by a fat woman whose husband, a Czech, was the chef. The place was old-fashioned, the food was plain and good; there was a regular clientele, very little conversation, and no – definitely no – muzak.

'Good holiday? Nice to see you back, Mr Wycliffe. Salad today: ham-off-the-bone or chicken.'

'I'll take the ham, Annie.'

In a world that was changing too fast for him Wycliffe clung to those things which survived as a drowning man clings to a plank.

He was glad to be alone. In a few hours he would be at the start of an intimate involvement with people he had never met who, for reasons often unconnected with any crime, would feel the need to lie. As usual, much of his investigation would be concerned with pinning down the innocent.

When he returned from lunch the internal telephone was ringing. It was Freda, the grey dragon who guarded the chief. 'Oh, Mr Wycliffe, if you are free, Mr Oldroyd would like a word, in his office.'

A trip along the corridor and through the padded door. Freda was amiable; she had her likes and dislikes which she made plain regardless of rank but Wycliffe was among her elect.

'Please go in, Mr Wycliffe.'

'Do sit down, Charles! I almost said "light up" – I can't get used to you without your pipe.'

Something tricky. Bertram Oldroyd was not given to beating about bushes. He sat in his swivel chair studying his finger nails then, abruptly: 'I suppose you've heard from Reed?'

'Just before lunch; I'm going down there shortly.'

'And I suppose you know Simon Lander?'

'The lawyer? . . . I've met him a few times on committees.' Wycliffe guessed what was coming but decided to let his chief sweat it out.

'Yes, well, Simon's got his long fingers in quite a few pies. Among others, as you must know, he's a member of the Police Authority. And they listen to him.'

Oldroyd looked over his glasses. 'He lives next door to the Bottrells on land that once belonged to the estate and the two families have been mixed up for generations. Anyway, Simon is worried, he's convinced that this Miller fellow committed suicide – says he's a strange sort of chap and that he's been very morose lately. Tom Reed has other ideas and he isn't being very communicative.'

'Should he be?'

Oldroyd smiled. 'Don't get testy, Charles! If there's been a crime Lander will want to get it sorted. Just form your own opinion and if you decide there's a case, tell him so.'

'But tactfully.'

Oldroyd looked at him with slightly narrowed eyes. 'Isn't that second nature to you, Charles?'

The message was clear: 'Watch your rear and don't rock the boat more than you have to.'

It was half-past five when Wycliffe arrived in the village, an uneasy mix of old cottages and modern bungalows with a pub and a church. A lane beside the pub was signposted: 'Duloe and Treave only. No throughway.' Duloe is Cornish for 'two inlets' and the estate is situated on a wooded promontory between two creeks of the River Fal.

Wycliffe drove along a poorly surfaced, narrow lane with no passing places. Fortunately, after three or four hundred yards it ended in a large circular space all but enclosed by a high stone wall backed by trees. Imposing granite pillars, green with moss and each surmounted by the effigy of a sleeping cat, marked the entrance to the estate, while nearby, in a more modest setting, a white-painted gate was labelled Treave.

Wycliffe passed between the pillars with their cats and down a long, rutted drive encroached upon by rhododendron and laurel. Once or twice, through the trees, he glimpsed the lower creek. Then, abruptly, he emerged from the gloom of the shrubbery into early evening sunshine, and there was the house. It was small as country houses go, a single rectangular block: two storeys of Georgian severity, the front relieved by a pillared portico and a balustraded terrace, probably added later. He parked on weedy gravel beside a patrol car and a police van. The house fronted on parkland grazed by sheep and studded with trees. The ground sloped easily to the river – a green channel between wooded banks.

Evening comes early to these river valleys and the light was already golden. A large motor launch loaded with trippers cruised upstream while a disembodied voice echoed between the slopes: 'On our left we have Duloe Estate, home of the Bottrell family since 1660. The present house was built at the beginning of the last century after a disastrous fire . . .'

The launch passed out of sight around the next bend and the voice was cut off as though by a switch. After that there was no sign of life anywhere, human or animal. The house stared with blind eyes across the valley and in this controlled and domesticated landscape Wycliffe experienced a strange sense of desolation. Then a uniformed copper came crunching towards him over the gravel.

'Mr Reed is at the cottage, sir . . . I'll show you.'

The constable escorted him around the front of the

house, past some outbuildings, and into a patch of woodland. In a clearing they came upon a typical Cornish cottage, stone-built and slate roofed. Ordinary enough, but transformed by its setting into a woodman's cottage out of Grimms' tales. The constable said: 'In the old days it belonged to the gamekeeper.'

Reed was alone in the living-room with the body. As senior CID officer for the sub-division he and Wycliffe were in frequent contact and it was not long since they had been involved together in a major case. Reed was a large man (stooping now to avoid the low beams), bald, except for a fringe of auburn hair; he had a fresh complexion and clear blue eyes of peculiar innocence.

Miller's body was there, sprawled in an armchair by the fireplace. A shotgun discharged at close range makes a mess; much of the man's neck and lower jaw were missing; only torn tissues and congealed blood remained, and this had spattered and dripped and dried on his clothing and on every adjacent surface.

'Whose gun is it?'

'His, sir.' Reed went on: 'I've moved nothing; our scenes-of-crime chap took his pictures without disturbing anything and the surgeon was careful.'

'What did the surgeon say about time of death?'

'He thought late yesterday evening or early morning, say between ten and two.' Reed rarely looked at the person to whom he was talking; one had the impression that his eyes were focused on some far horizon.

Because of the barrel length (and this one was unusually long) it is difficult to commit suicide with a shotgun. The problem is sometimes solved by attaching a piece of string to the trigger. In this instance the string had been passed under the victim's right instep so that the pull was in the right direction.

'What makes you suspect murder?'

Reed's eyes focused briefly on Wycliffe. 'Two things. First the string is too short; he couldn't have reached the string any more than he could have reached the trigger.'

It was true. Wycliffe stooped, picked up the end of the string, and drew it taut; it came inches short of the probable reach of the dead man's fingers.

'You said there were two things.'

A smile appeared on Reed's lips. 'I discovered that Miller was left-handed but the trigger string passes under his right instep – obviously for a right-handed person.'

'So the killer was trying to cover his tracks by rigging a suicide but he wasn't very good at it.'

Reed nodded. 'It looks to me like an unpremeditated crime and the killer was in a panic when he tried to improvise.'

Wycliffe was noncommittal. 'I gather Lander still thinks he killed himself.'

'Yes. It seems Miller arrived back from a holiday on Friday – sooner than expected, and very depressed. Lander thinks something must have happened while he was away.'

'What sort of chap was he? Do we know anything about him?'

'Not a lot. He seems to have been an unusual type for an estate foreman. He came here four or five years ago in answer to an advertisement in *The Countryman*, and that's about it, so far.'

'He lived here alone?'

'For the most part but, looking around upstairs, I get the impression he might have had company from time to time.'

'Are there any relatives?'

'Lander knows of none.'

Wycliffe brooded on the young man, now horribly disfigured in death. In life he must have been presentable:

he was fair, his features fine and sensitive – what could be seen of them. His eyes were disturbing – naturally, because they were open and staring, but Wycliffe thought that even in life they might have caused a tremor of disquiet. A good figure with no spare flesh, five-ten or eleven. What had persuaded him to bury himself in this place while still a young man?

On the table, within his easy reach, was a gleaming flute, now spattered with dried blood. The case was open beside it.

'It seems he played a lot – mainly to himself.'

Wycliffe said: 'The pathologist should be here soon and I've got a ballistics man coming to take a look at him before he's shifted.'

The living-room seemed to confirm the image already forming in his mind: the furniture had probably changed little since the gamekeeper's day but there were improvised shelves stacked with books, mainly paperbacks, ranging from classical and modern fiction to works on history, philosophy and psychology. There were framed contemporary prints on the walls, and a sophisticated audio box of tricks with racks of tapes and compact discs.

Indeed an unusual estate foreman.

Reed said: 'Do you want what little I've got in the way of background, sir? So far I've talked to Lander and his daughter, and I've had a brief word with his lordship. Apart from the girl's statement about finding the body there have been no formal interviews.'

'I'll take a look round before getting too involved.'

Wycliffe went through to the kitchen: a bottled-gas stove, running hot-and-cold water, and a fridge – the essentials but no frills. Under the sink there was a wine rack half-full of bottles. One end of the kitchen was screened off and fitted with a hand-basin and a shower cabinet. The whole place had an air of positive neatness and cleanliness, more to be expected of a rather fussy spinster than a youngish bachelor.

He went back to the living-room and up the narrow, creaking stairs. Two doors opened off a tiny landing. The first led into a small bedroom, little more than a cell. There was a single bed, a chest of drawers, a shelf of books, and a curtained-off corner for hanging clothes. On the chest there was a clock-radio. As in the downstairs rooms it was adequate – no more.

The other bedroom was larger, with a double bed, wardrobe, tallboy, and washstand – more relics of the gamekeeper's day. The room was apparently unused though the bed was made up.

He returned downstairs and joined Reed, standing outside in the filtered sunshine. Reed said: 'Odd, isn't it? Looks as though he kept that room for when he had company.' He added: 'I think we're about to have company ourselves, sir; I heard a car.'

'That will be Fox.'

Wycliffe's scenes-of-crime officer was lean and long-legged, with a receding chin, an obtrusive nose, and a certain hesitancy in his walk – like a discriminating stork. He arrived with his assistant, loaded with gear from his van which could not be brought close to the cottage. Fox had the job of putting the scene of crime on record through scale drawings, photographs and inventories. This he would do superbly well – missing nothing, but, as Wycliffe once remarked, 'Only Fox could be surrounded by trees without knowing that he was in a wood.'

At this stage Wycliffe liked to spend time familiarizing himself with the location and with the people, without taking aboard too much detail. Leaving the cottage to Reed and to Fox he walked back towards the big house. Even by Cornish standards for country houses Duloe was not large; it was pleasantly situated in a few acres of park and woodland with adjoining farms. There were no formal gardens, no Grecian temples; no fountains and no nymphs. It had never been one of the 'great houses'; now it had the appearance of a small estate slipping gently into decay.

He reached the house and climbed the broad steps to the terrace where weeds sprouted between the paving slabs. Looking up at the pediment he saw again the effigy of a sleeping cat – this time carved in relief and with an inscription, just legible: 'Innocens et Necesse'.

'Harmless and necessary.' A voice from behind him. 'Filched from *The Merchant of Venice* – Shylock and his "harmless and necessary cat".'

Wycliffe turned to face the speaker.

'Commending my ancestor for a barony, in 1795, Pitt said that he had made himself "harmless and necessary to government for thirty years". The first Baron Bottrell promptly adopted the phrase as his motto and the cat as his emblem.'

'A sleeping cat?'

A quick smile. 'Simply with closed eyes. Isn't that essential to being harmless? You, I take it, are Charles Wycliffe . . . Hugh Bottrell. I'm so glad you've been able to come down and look into this terrible affair.'

The Ninth Baron was suave, polished, and probably in his early fifties, but athletic, slender and supple; he had a good crop of dark hair turning grey and even his jeans and cotton tunic were worn with distinction.

'Would it trouble you to give me a few minutes of your time, Mr Wycliffe? . . . Come inside.'

Wycliffe followed him through an empty entrance hall, down a dimly lit corridor, to a room at the back of the house. By contrast with what he had seen so far this room was light, cheerful and welcoming. French windows opened to a paved courtyard and, in the courtyard, a weeping ash filtered the evening sunshine. Chintzes, in which greens and mauves predominated, helped to merge indoors with out.

'My wife, Cynthia . . . Chief Superintendent Wycliffe.'

Cynthia Bottrell was younger than her husband, probably still under forty; an elegant woman, sleek and blonde, who knew how to dress to give herself the height she lacked.

A restrained smile and the touch of a cool hand: 'Do sit down.'

The only possible dog for Lady Bottrell – an English setter – spread its elegance over the carpet in a pool of sunshine by the window. It turned a brown unwinking eye on Wycliffe but otherwise did not disturb itself.

Bottrell seated himself in a corner of a large settee, one arm spread along the back, legs crossed. 'I thought we might help to put you in the picture.'

Wycliffe said nothing and Bottrell continued: 'Tony Miller was employed as an estate foreman but he was altogether a superior person, well read, fond of music . . .'

'Then why—'

'Why come here to a more or less menial job?' Bottrell interrupted, smooth as whipped cream. 'I suppose because he wanted to live in the country, because it suited him to have a house to himself, and because like many young men today he shirked responsibility. He came here five years ago on a two-way trial; he liked us and we liked him, so he stayed.'

'Did he have any particular friends?'

'As far as I know he had no enemies. Reed's notion that he was murdered seems to me fantastic.'

Lady Bottrell, serene and decorative in a bergère chair, intervened for the first time. 'But that is not an answer to the question, Hugh. Tony had friends, Mr Wycliffe, if one cares to call them that. He was gay, and inclined to be promiscuous.' Her manner was oddly incisive, perhaps spiteful.

Bottrell snapped: 'You exaggerate, Cynthia!' But immediately modified his tone. 'I'm sorry, my dear, but Tony is dead and one is reluctant to speak ill of him.'

Wycliffe was realizing that almost everything in the rooom had seen better days: the carpet was threadbare in places, the wallpaper faded, the upholstery worn. The pictures on the walls were all modern prints except for a single gilt-framed portrait in oils of an elderly man in full regalia.

'My grandfarther,' Bottrell said, 'in his coronation robes.'

And on a pier table below the picture, silver framed, was a photograph of the young queen signed: 'Elizabeth R'.

They were interrupted by a new arrival, unmistakably another Bottrell male. The man came in from the courtyard and stood just inside the room, looking about him. 'I thought I left a book here . . . I was sitting where you are, Hugh. It could have slipped between the cushions . . .'

Bottrell got up. 'My brother, James, Dr Bottrell . . . Mr Wycliffe . . . Superintendent Wycliffe is here to look into the circumstances of Tony's death.'

James Bottrell carried more weight than his brother, his features were heavier, his body slacker, his manner more sombre and deliberate. He wore a khaki shirt and crumpled corded trousers. He was lame, dragging his left leg and holding it stiff as though from a knee injury.

Routing among the cushions of the settee he acknowledged his brother's introduction with a casual glance in Wycliffe's direction. 'Really? I wish you joy.' Then, to his sister-in-law: 'You haven't seen my book, Cynthia? – Hurwitz and Christiansen – I'm sure I left it here . . .' And after an unproductive pause: 'Damn it, it's big enough!'

Lord Bottrell looked at Wycliffe in mild embarrassment but his wife was untroubled. 'You need a secretary, James – or a nursemaid.'

Defeated, Dr Bottrell left by the way he had come.

Cynthia turned to Wycliffe with a smile. 'James is my husband's twin; but he had the luck – good or bad – to be second on the scene. He's a psychologist and not long ago he resigned a consultancy to come here and write a book on the criminal mind or something of the sort.' Lady Bottrell's manner was amused and tolerant. 'He has a sort of lair in the old stables where he lives, only emerging in search of meals, lost books, or spectacles.'

Lord Bottrell said: 'James has the brains of the family.'

Wycliffe, though pleased with these insights into family life, felt the need at this stage to be single minded: 'Getting back to Miller, I understand that he had only recently returned from holiday.'

'That's right. He came back on Friday though he wasn't due until Sunday. Something quite serious must have happened to upset him; he wasn't at all himself.'

'Do you know where he spent his holiday?'

'He didn't say; he was rather a secretive sort of chap.'

The telephone rang and Lady Bottrell reached for the receiver without moving from her chair. 'Duloe House. Cynthia Bottrell speaking . . .' She turned to Wycliffe. 'It's for you.'

It was Reed, speaking from the cottage. 'Dr Franks is here, sir.'

Reluctantly, Wycliffe left. Lord Bottrell followed him on to the terrace. 'Come at any time . . .' And then with a certain diffidence: 'First impressions can be deceptive.'

A thought occurred to Wycliffe: 'I shall have to talk to Lander and to his daughter; can you put me in the picture about the Lander household?'

Did his lordship resent the question? There was a significant pause before he said: 'I can tell you something, I suppose. Simon's father is still alive and lives with them. Then there is Jean – she is sixteen and, of course, her mother, Beth.'

Wycliffe thanked him and walked off towards the cottage, brooding. He was puzzled; he had a feeling that he had been treated to a piece of theatre. The Bottrells were acting, though not to an agreed script. But he knew better than to conclude that this had any necessary connection with the crime. Lift any stone . . .

Shortly after leaving the house he met a young man – a boy, coming up from the direction of the river. The boy wore swimming trunks and flip-flop sandals, and his hair was wet. Another Bottrell? No doubt, the future Tenth Baron. For a moment it looked as though the boy might stop and speak but he did not.

When Lord Bottrell returned to his wife's sitting-room she was out in the courtyard watering her potted plants. As he joined her she said, without turning round: 'You're on thin ice, darling.'

'You think so? He seems a decent sort; not looking for trouble, I'd say. But you weren't exactly helpful.'

She went to a tap to refill her watering can. 'One had to give him something. You don't think you could have stopped them finding out that Tony was gay? Everybody in the village knows and when the press gets hold of it so will a few million others.'

'I don't see much in this for the press.'

She turned to look at him. 'With a peer involved? Don't be so naive, Hugh!'

For a while Cynthia went on with her watering and Bottrell stood watching, half hoping, half afraid that she had not said all she intended.

It came at last. 'I wish you weren't so mixed up with Lander.'

'Lander? But he's our solicitor. How can I avoid, as you say, being "mixed up with him"?'

Cynthia turned to look at her husband. 'Don't treat me like a fool, Hugh! I don't know what all this is about; I'm not sure if you do. In any case I don't want to know. But the police are asking who killed Miller, and why? They'll keep on asking until they find out. Sooner or later they'll get on to the Biddick girl. They may or may not be interested in what she has to tell but the press certainly will be and Lizzie Biddick is not a girl to turn down a good offer.'

'I don't know why you bring her into it.'

'Don't you? I wonder.'

Wycliffe found Franks waiting for him, sunning himself at the cottage door. The two had worked together on almost every homicide in the region for twenty years. Their temperaments were decidedly incompatible; Franks opposed a cheerful cynicism to Wycliffe's rather gloomy fatalism. That they got on as well as they did was largely due to the pathologist's good humour and tolerance.

'This is awkward, Charles; I know these people.'

'Which people?'

'The Bottrells, damn it! I occasionally go sailing with Hugh.'

'What's that got to do with it? Your job is to give an opinion on how this poor devil died, not to sit in judgement on anybody.'

Franks looked at him with speculative eyes. 'Sometimes I wonder about you, Charles.'

'It's mutual.'

They went inside. Reed and Fox could be heard moving about upstairs. Franks bent over the body in the chair.

'I don't want him shifted yet; I've got Melville coming down to give an opinion on the possibility or otherwise of suicide from the ballistics point of view.'

Franks turned to him. 'You still have doubts?'

'Let's say I don't want any arguments from the lawyers if and when this comes to court.'

'Well, if I can't shift him what do you want me to tell you – that he's dead?'

'Melville should be here at any minute; I was expecting him before you.'

Franks looked at his watch and sighed.

A man stood in the doorway; he was small, sharp-featured with tiny eyes bright and restless as a squirrel's. 'Gentlemen!' His eyes took in the room, then he went over to stand by the dead man. 'So nothing's been moved. I take it I'm free to examine the weapon?'

'DS Fox, the scenes-of-crime officer, is upstairs; I would like you to work with him.'

Fox came down and Wycliffe joined Franks outside.

Franks said: 'Old Melville is a fusspot. I hope he won't be all night.'

'What's your opinion of Lord Bottrell?'

'As somebody to go sailing with he's a very pleasant companion. He's not one of the world's brains, but no fool either.'

'You've met his wife?'

'Naturally; a very attractive woman.'

'But?'

Franks grinned. 'Too much the dominant female for my taste. I fancy she's more mother than mistress to our

Hugh. But she fits in at Duloe, the perfect chatelaine; you'd think she was born to it.'

'And wasn't she?'

'Her father has a smallholding down the river. I've been told that most Wednesdays you can find him in Truro market hanging about waiting for somebody to buy him a drink.'

'What about the brother – Bottrell's brother?'

'I've never met him but we've corresponded.'

'About what?'

Franks drew a quick breath. 'You are a wonder, Charles! Why the hell should I tell you all this about people who are friends of mine?'

'No reason at all, but you will.'

'He's asked my professional opinion a couple of times on cases he wants to discuss in a book he's writing on criminal psychology.'

'I gather there's a son and heir.'

'Yes, Paul; he's sixteen; a nice lad – quiet, studious, doesn't give much of himself away.'

'Thanks; that puts me in the picture.'

'Don't you want to know about the Frog?'

'The Frog?'

'Lander – that's what everybody calls him.'

Wycliffe recalled that Lander's thin-lipped mouth seemed to stretch almost from ear to ear.

'Does he go sailing with his lordship?'

'Only when his lordship can't shake him off politely. Lander has all the compelling charm of toothache on a wet Sunday. Apart from that I only know that he's supposed to be a good estate lawyer. Certainly Hugh won't turn around without asking him first. Sometimes I get the impression that Lander works him by strings.'

'The place doesn't look exactly prosperous.'

'You can say that again! Hugh has Marks and Spencer,

ICI, and a few others, to thank for still being here. His grandfather made some shrewd investments back in the twenties and early thirties. Without them Duloe would now be a theme park or something equally bloody.'

They chatted for a while before Melville joined them.

'I would like to take the weapon back with me. If you will have it tagged and logged I'll give you a receipt.' The little man was a model of crisp efficiency.

Reed who had remained in the background through all this did what was necessary.

Wycliffe said: 'You've formed some opinion?'

Melville pursed his lips. 'It's obvious to anybody that the charge was bunched, indicating that the weapon was fired at close range.'

'But how close? Consistent with it being held between the thighs with the muzzle in contact with the neck or under the chin?'

'Almost certainly the muzzle was in contact with the neck – the neck rather than the chin . . .' Melville paused, his expression full of doubt and caution. 'I can't be definite but my impression is that the weapon at the time of discharge was not in a more or less vertical position as it would have been if gripped between the man's thighs with the butt on the floor.'

'So can you suggest any scenario that would account for the injuries as you see them?'

Melville stood first on one leg, then on the other. 'I don't want to commit myself. Deceased was certainly sitting or sprawled in his chair when the gun was discharged. Beyond that . . .'

Experts tend to be cocooned in their expertise and anything beyond bald fact has to be prized out of them. Wycliffe was brusque.

'Unless you are prepared to go further than that, you have told us no more than is obvious.'

The brown eyes flicked from Wycliffe to Franks and back again. 'Well, if I have to be more specific I would say that the deceased could have been threatened while on his feet; he could have retreated and fallen or slumped into the chair, then his assailant might have brought the muzzle of the shotgun into contact with his neck, forcing the head back, and fired . . .'

'So you would discount the idea of suicide?'

'What I have seen is, I believe, inconsistent with suicide.'

The little man was thanked and sent on his way with the shotgun in a polythene wrapper.

Wycliffe said: 'I can imagine what counsel would do to him.'

Franks began his examination of the body while Fox made a photographic record of every stage.

While they were at it two men arrived with a stretcher-trolley to take the body away.

Franks glanced at his watch. 'God! It's half-seven. Well, that's it, then! I'm hoping to get dinner in Truro; what are you doing?'

'I don't know; they've arranged something. But what have you got to tell me?'

Franks looked from Wycliffe to the body. 'About him? What do you expect? You know that he's dead, you know that he was shot, and you know when. The rest is in your province. Anyway I'll give you a ring when I've had a chance to look at him on the table . . . Sure you won't come with me for a meal?'

Under Reed's supervision the men removed Tony Miller's body, carrying it to their van parked on the outskirts of the little wood.

Chapter Three

When the body had been taken away Wycliffe said: 'It's getting late, we'll pack up for the night and carry on in the morning.'

Fox looked at him in injured protest. 'But we've just started, sir!'

Wycliffe was indifferent. 'It's up to you.' He turned to Reed. 'I shall want a man here to keep an eye on the place overnight.' And then: 'You probably haven't had more than a snack since breakfast; what about coming along to the pub with me? Incidentally, did they book me in there?'

'Yes, sir. I only hope you'll be comfortable.'

They went to the village in Reed's car and an hour later they came out of the pub dining-room into the warm darkness. People were sitting at tables outside, talking in low voices.

Wycliffe said: 'See you in the morning; I think I'll go for a walk.'

Without consciously making any decision he set off down the lane towards Duloe. The silence was absolute until an owl hooted and a pale form passed soundlessly within a few feet of his head. Away to his left he could see the glare in the sky from the lights of Truro. It was the darkness of a moonless summer night when only detail and colours are missing.

He was in a strange mood – detached, irresponsible; he could not take seriously this case in which he had so readily involved himself; perhaps it had been no more than an excuse to avoid the routine of the office for a day or two longer. And yet, so it seemed, a man had been murdered.

As he approached the entrance to the estate he noticed a small house away to his right, well back from the lane. He could see its shadowy outline against the sky, box-like and stark. There was a light in a downstairs room and the sound of pop music reached him, muffled and throbbing.

He arrived in the broad open space at the end of the lane. The white gate of Treave stood out, and beyond he could see the lights of the house. The pillars at the entrance to Duloe loomed but the drive itself was soon swallowed up in darkness. Somewhere a fox barked, briefly imperative.

Perhaps it was the setting. But there was something of unreality about the people too: the Ninth Baron, trying a little too hard to be all things to all men; his wife, elegant in her once charming sitting-room, seated in her bergère chair, while her father cadged drinks at the weekly cattle market; his lordship's brother, apparently obsessed by his study of the criminal mind and, finally, the young Apollo, the heir presumptive.

Outside the family, the dead man, the superior estate foreman who was supposed to have shot himself. 'A promiscuous gay,' said her ladyship. Bitterness there. And the lawyer – Lander, whom Franks had nominated as his lordship's puppet-master.

Wycliffe brought his watch close to his eyes: half-past nine. Why not? His call would be unexpected, probably resented, and that could be an advantage.

He pushed open the white gate. He could see the house in silhouette, low, with interesting roof profiles, tall chimneys, and gables. He crunched down the gravelled drive and started a dog barking in the house. The front door was set in a broad, arched alcove; he pressed the bell. There was light in the room to the left of the front door. Another came on over his head and he was conscious of being inspected through a small glass panel in the door. The door opened.

A frosty, 'Yes?'

It was Lander himself, lean and gaunt and petulant. The dog, a black and white collie, was held by its collar.

'Chief Superintendent Wycliffe. I know that this is an unreasonable time to call but in the circumstances . . .'

From the hall, Wycliffe could hear a television in the lighted room, and the door was ajar. He realized that he was about to be shunted elsewhere for a tête-à-tête with the lawyer which had probably been rehearsed. This was not what he had in mind and with that effrontery which good policemen can carry off to order he pushed the door wide and left Lander no alternative but to follow him in.

'I'm very sorry to disturb you . . .'

The television was showing a play; two people had been watching; a woman and a young girl. Lander made the best of the situation.

Now that he could see the man clearly Wycliffe realized that, if not actually drunk, he was affected by drink; his eyes had a glazed look, his movements were too deliberate and his speech unduly precise.

'Chief Superintendent Wycliffe . . . My wife, Beth, my daughter, Jean . . .'

The television was switched off. Lander saw Wycliffe seated and returned to the chair he had recently left. On a small table at his elbow there was a whisky glass, one-third full.

A 'period' room belonging to no period; a white ceiling with exposed beams; a high wainscot, then a shelf with an array of willow-patterned plates and dishes; it was reminiscent of certain hotel dining-rooms where it all comes with the carpet.

'A whisky, Mr Wycliffe?'

Wycliffe declined. 'There are just one or two points I would like to deal with informally and at first hand.'

'What a strange time to call!' Beth Lander, acid, deprived of her play. She was auburn-haired with pale, freckled skin; her hair was scraped back into an absurd pony-tail, drawing attention to her rather pinched features and to her slightly protruding eyes.

Lander coughed and sipped his whisky.

The girl, Jean, her long legs cased in tight jeans, her feet bare, remained curled up in an armchair. Her father glared at her but she seemed not to notice. She was attractive; pale like her mother, but she had a mop of red hair, and incisive features, well composed; a Rossetti girl. Wycliffe noticed that her eyes were slightly swollen; tears had been shed not so long ago. Sixteen, Bottrell had said.

There was a brittle silence while they waited for him to begin. He turned to Lander: 'Apart from the conditions in which he was found, Mr Lander, what makes you so sure that Miller killed himself?'

Lander, like a man emerging from anaesthesia, coming to grips, mustered some slight aggression: 'The circumstances . . . Surely if you find a man with a shotgun between his thighs and the muzzle at his neck—'

Wycliffe interrupted: 'I said, apart from those circumstances. I gather from Mr Reed that you were not greatly surprised.'

'Of course I was surprised!' Lander spluttered in his agitation. 'Is Reed saying that I expected the man to kill himself? . . . What I said was that he came back from his holiday before time, very depressed. Lord Bottrell remarked on it . . . Something must have happened . . .'

His voice trailed off, the thread of his argument apparently lost.

Watching Lander talk at any time must have been a distracting experience; whenever he opened his mouth his face seemed almost to split in two.

Wycliffe said: 'I'm afraid the indications are that Miller was murdered, and that makes his early return and his depression even more important. Have you any idea where he spent his holiday?'

Lander took a sip of whisky and put the glass down. 'You're sure you won't join me? . . . No? . . . I've no idea where he went.'

'And he gave you no indication of what had upset him?'

This was too much for Lander; he snapped: 'My dear Wycliffe, I was not in the man's confidence!'

'I'm told that he was homosexual and inclined to be promiscuous.'

Lander suppressed a too hasty retort and said, simply: 'I know nothing of his private life.'

Before the cock crows twice? . . . At any rate Lander's protests were unconvincingly vehement.

'To your knowledge, did he have people to stay at his cottage?'

'I don't know about people staying there but he had visitors. I've no knowledge of who they were or what his relationships with them might have been.'

Beth Lander had been following the exchange, her eyes on one speaker, then the other; now she asked: 'So you are quite certain that Miller was murdered?'

'That is where the evidence points, Mrs Lander.'

'Is it the case that gays who are unfaithful to their partners run a greater risk of jealous revenge than people who are sexually normal?'

It was Wycliffe's turn to be taken off balance. 'I'm afraid I've no data on which to judge.'

'That is what I have read, but Dr Bottrell says there is no evidence to support it.'

Lander, more than ever ill at ease, and trying hard to follow the exchange, said: 'Lord Bottrell's brother is an authority on the psychology of crime.' He made it sound like wife beating.

A straw in the wind? Mixing the metaphor, human motives are so complex that a poor copper, searching desperately for a lead, is accustomed to find himself up the proverbial creek. All the same, he was intrigued by the woman's question.

He wanted to involve the daughter, who had not yet opened her mouth. Try something banal: 'You had a very distressing experience this morning, Miss Lander.'

She looked startled, and shifted her feet off the chair to sit normally. For her, the situation had become formal.

'You were taking the dog for a walk, I believe?'

'Jean has made a full statement, Superintendent,' Lander said.

'I know, but I haven't had a chance to read it. What time was it, approximately?'

'Half-past eight? I don't know exactly – it was quite early.'

'Your walk took you through the spinney, past Miller's cottage?'

'It's a short cut from our garden through to the estate.'

'And you wanted to walk in the estate.'

Lander said: 'We wander at will, Superintendent. Without referring to a map I doubt if any of us could say where our land ends and Duloe land begins.'

Wycliffe ignored him. 'You often go that way?'

'Sometimes.'

She was tense, but her answers came almost casually, like a well-learned lesson. Was it the questions she anticipated which troubled her?

'The door of the cottage was open?'

'Yes.'

'Your dog ran in and you followed – is that correct?'

'Yes.'

The girl was lying. Years of experience had nurtured a sixth sense in these matters and he was probing close to the nerve. She was leaning forward, looking at him as though mesmerized and gripping her knees with her fingers.

Deliberately he offered her an escape route: 'You knew Tony Miller pretty well?'

The tension relaxed; a dangerous corner negotiated; she almost sighed with relief. 'Yes, I suppose so.'

'What did you think of him?'

She looked surprised. 'I don't know. He was a bit odd. I can't say I thought about him much.'

That was candid; he believed true; but there was something very wrong. He was puzzled; he could understand the girl being distressed, but not afraid. He would have to take it further but not now with Lander breathing down his neck.

As though on cue somebody opened the door; a thin, elderly man stood in the doorway. 'Ah! I didn't know you had someone here.'

Lander said: 'This is Chief Superintendent Wycliffe . . . Meet my father, Mr Wycliffe . . .'

The old man shook hands more at ease than his son. They had the same build and similar features, but a white, straggling moustache helped to hide in the father the wide mouth so conspicuous in his son.

Wycliffe, having stood up, remained standing.

'You are here about young Miller?'

'Yes, sir. We've come to the conclusion that he was murdered.'

A slow nod. 'So I understand.' He seemed about to

add something but changed his mind and finished: 'You've got a problem on your hands, Mr Wycliffe.'

Beth Lander got up from her chair. 'I'll make your cocoa, Father.'

The mantel clock chimed: a quarter past ten. Wycliffe apologized for intruding. 'I must be getting along to my hotel.'

Simon Lander asked: 'Are you staying overnight?'

'I'm booked in at the village pub.'

Lander looked disapproving. 'At the pub? You'll find it's pretty basic.'

'I expect I shall survive.'

Wycliffe let himself out by the white gate with a sense of relief, almost of having escaped. A certain tension was to be expected but in all his dealings with families he had rarely experienced such an awareness of separate individuals between whom there was no common ground, no accord; only suspicion and hostility. Grandfather, father, mother, and daughter were continuing to live together in the same house long after all but the most conventional bonds had disappeared. It was not what they had said or done, it was a matter of attitude, of atmosphere . . .

As Lander returned to the drawing-room his daughter brushed past him without a word and he heard her going upstairs. The room was empty. He was about to switch on the television but changed his mind; what he did and said when Beth returned from making his father's bedtime drink would be critical. At all costs he must maintain the status quo; no sharp words, no clever repartee; he must be calm, kind, and reasonable; eminently reasonable. He finished his whisky but did not sit down. He was going to pour himself another but decided not to. That bloody man! He hadn't come to ask questions, he'd come to stir the pot. And he'd chosen his time!

He heard heavy steps on the stairs: his father going up to bed, then Beth in the hall. She came in. 'Where's Jean?'

'Gone up to her room.'

Beth busied herself gathering up newspapers and magazines and returning them to the rack. Without looking at him she demanded: 'What was all that about?'

'They think Miller was murdered.'

'I understood that; I'm not stupid. What puzzles me is why you pretended to think differently.'

'I—'

'It doesn't matter. What was wrong with Jean?'

'Naturally she was upset, being questioned by Wycliffe. It was quite disgraceful – coming here at night and subjecting the girl—'

'Have you finished with this?' In her tidying she had picked up his empty whisky glass.

He was still confused and she was deliberately harassing him; he would have liked to slap her, but he swallowed hard. 'Yes . . . Yes, I—'

His wife went on: 'You had her crying in your study earlier. What was that about?'

She was looking at him now, her head thrust forward, her hair scraped back, forehead and cheek bones shining, eyes staring . . . He thought: My God. Why did I ever . . . ? But he forced himself to speak calmly. 'I knew that she was lying . . . I know lies when I hear them.'

'Oh, you're an expert on lies; I'll give you that. But what was she lying about?' She raised her voice. 'What about?'

Lander went to stand by the fireplace, his back to the room. Perhaps because he did not want to see his wife he spoke over his shoulder. 'You don't know what your daughter has been up to. On Sunday night, when you thought she was in bed, she was out with young Paul. She was out at one in the morning – one in the morning, mind you! She went out after we thought she'd gone to bed . . . That's what she was lying about.'

'And you made her tell you that. How very clever of you! And you made her cry into the bargain. You are a natural bully, Simon!' She spat it out. 'You're also drunk. Do you think Wycliffe didn't see it?'

'I still haven't told you . . .'

'What haven't you told me?'

'It doesn't matter.' He was feeling slightly more sure of himself, on safer ground; she had, he thought, been diverted from the Miller theme.

He was wrong. In a calmer voice she said: 'What is this Miller business about, Simon? Does that girl come into it?'

'What girl?' He sounded hoarse.

'Don't treat me like a fool! What happened to her?'

He made an effort to compose himself. 'If you are talking about the Biddick girl, she left. You must know that.'

'Sudden, wasn't it?'

'I don't know about that. She gave in her notice, and went. You can ask Cynthia.'

His wife was silent for so long that he turned to face her. She was looking at him, her eyes so coldly speculative that he was disturbed. She said in a level, unemotional voice: 'Up to now I've never troubled about your little games but if you're mixed up in this then you had better watch out.'

He was alarmed; he had never known her either so bitter or so self-confident, usually she took refuge in hysterical weeping. 'I don't know what you're talking about, Beth. What am I supposed to have done? Unless you tell me—'

She cut him short. 'No, Simon! It is you who will start telling me if we are to talk at all.'

'But what do I tell? You know what there is to know!'

He stood there, staring at her, the great gape of his mouth exposing too many teeth and she turned away. 'It doesn't matter. We shall see.'

That night Wycliffe lay long awake pondering on the people he had met for the first time that evening. The Bottrells. On the face of it they were a family like any other but in truth they were very different, survivors of a threatened species, like his countess in the Dordogne. For three centuries Bottrells had lived at Duloe, managing the same land, handing on their privileges and obligations from father to son, with a vested interest in continuity, resisting and wrestling with change.

Wycliffe told himself: 'My father was a small-time farmer, I'm a policeman, my son is a scientist working for the UN in Kenya, but Paul Bottrell, by the grace of God and the stock market, will one day take up the family struggle as the Tenth Baron.'

And the Landers had much in common with the Bottrells: for six or seven generations they had practised law in the county town; for the whole of that time they had acted as estate lawyers for the Bottrells, and for ninety years they had lived in a house, built on land once part of the estate.

Wycliffe tossed and tumbled in his bed trying to grasp what such continuity meant, how it affected the attitudes and responses of the two families to the fluid society in which they now found themselves; dinosaurs who have outlived their strange forests and mighty swamps.

At last he fell asleep, a small smile on his lips, muttering: 'How long is a piece of string?'

Chapter Four

He awoke in daylight, not knowing where he was. For a moment it seemed that he had gone back in time; the sloping ceiling with exposed beams and the dormer window reminded him of the farmhouse bedroom which had been his in childhood. Then he noticed the faint smell of beer which pervades every corner in any pub and he was fully awake. He got out of bed and crossed to the window. The church was only yards away, the width of the pub car park. Beyond that he could see the roofs of a few houses, then fields and trees with just a glimpse of the river in the middle distance. He put on a dressing gown and went in search of the bathroom.

Lander had warned him that facilities would be basic. It wasn't four-star but there was a shower with plenty of hot water. Back in his bedroom, he dressed. He was fussy about his clothes, especially during a murder inquiry; he had no wish to look like an undertaker or even a manager for Marks and Spencer, but he believed that relatives of the deceased were entitled to a certain restraint. Years ago he had settled for a lightweight grey check, very subdued, though Helen still claimed he looked like a bookie. With this suit he wore a matching fisherman's hat. The outfit was renewed as required and Helen hoped in vain that the pattern would be discontinued.

At half-past seven he went downstairs. The door of the bar was open to the street and the landlord, in singlet, trousers and slippers, was smoking his first cigarette of the day and taking the morning air. The bar cat performed the intimate contortions of her toilet on the step beside him. In the dining area the kitchen door was open and Wycliffe could see the landlady at her stove; bacon sizzled in the pan and the smell made his mouth water.

She turned towards him. 'Egg and bacon – is that all right?'

'Fine.' Helen would not have approved of that either.

'A sausage?'

'Why not?'

She was fiftyish, plump, and wrapped around in a spotless white overall.

'I've only got you and a young couple in at the moment. We've cut down on what we used to do – taking it a bit easier now we're getting older. Bert – that's my husband – tells me you're here to look into things down at the House.'

It was one way of putting it.

'Come in and pour yourself some coffee if you want to. The pot's there on the hotplate and there's cups in the rack. This won't be long now.'

Wycliffe poured himself a cup of coffee.

'Jill Christophers, the housekeeper at Duloe, is my half-sister. She's quite a bit younger than me . . . A funny business. O'course Jill never talks about the family but you can tell. And that Miller – I know he's dead and one shouldn't speak ill of the dead but he was a strange one – never had much to say, but it was the way he looked – his eyes!' She glanced through the doorway into the dining area where there was movement. 'Oh, they're down, I wasn't expecting them just yet . . .'

Wycliffe retreated. The young couple were already seated at table and they looked at him with sufficient interest to show that they had been told who he was.

One of them had switched on the television. Breakfast TV was one of his pet hates – all that plastic *bonhomie* to go with the cornflakes. Now they were presenting a species of news. The Magellan space craft was probing the clouded secrets of the planet Venus, the ultimate in global warming; there was trouble in the Gulf; and the drug barons in Colombia had shot a member of their government. Set all that against the murder of an estate foreman. Simple, ordinary murder no longer shocked, so it was no longer news. Sometimes he wondered if it was becoming respectable.

But despite the television he enjoyed his breakfast and by eight-thirty he was at the cottage where Fox had arrived ahead of him.

The living-room looked as though the removal men were expected at any minute. Fox, with his half-glasses well down his nose, and his head held back to see through them, was seated at the desk going through its contents.

'Anything to tell me?'

Fox stood up, removed his glasses, and switched to his lecture mode: 'Judging by the prints I have so far recorded, sir, I would say that there have been two men, other than Miller, in the cottage fairly recently. One of them at least was a frequent visitor; his prints are scattered about and they seem to cover a considerable span of time.'

'How recent is fairly? Yesterday?'

'No, sir. Apart from the dead man's I've found none that seem to me as recent as that. Of course I have the upstairs rooms still to do.'

'Any more?'

'Yes; there is a fair sprinkling belonging to a woman who seems to have been a regular visitor also, but none of them are fresh. At a guess I'd say she hasn't been in the cottage for some days at least.'

Various items were laid out on the desk top. There was a ledger-type book with columns in which Miller listed jobs to be done, the date of completion, receipt of invoice and so on. There was a duplicate order book and a file for invoices labelled 'To Office'.

'Nothing of a personal nature?'

Fox opened one of the drawers with the flourish of a magician opening his magic box. He lifted out a wad of bank statements and a cheque book. The statements were unexciting; they told the hackneyed tale of a man living just within his income; Mr Micawber's recipe for happiness.

'Any letters?'

'None, sir. Nothing to indicate any connections he might have had away from this place except this.' Fox produced a recent hotel bill from the Crown Hotel, Dorchester, covering a four-night stay with certain meals.

So that was where he had spent his foreshortened holiday.

It was early days but Wycliffe was impressed by the man's anonymity, the apparent absence of roots. 'Send his dabs to CRO, with a description and, if you can find one, a photograph. If not, follow up with one of yours of the body.'

'You think he's got form, sir?'

'I don't think anything; it's routine.'

It was clear that Fox had not said all that was in his mind and it came out just as Wycliffe was about to leave: 'I don't quite know how to put this, sir; there's no evidence I can put my finger on – it's just a hunch, but I think somebody has been here before me.'

Fox having hunches was a welcome change. Usually he

suffered from a sad deficiency of ingredient X. But Wycliffe knew what he was talking about: anybody accustomed to making systematic searches acquires a sixth sense about coming second on the scene. It may be an unnatural tidiness or the absence of personal idiosyncracies in the way things are stowed, supplemented, in this case, by the fact that so little of a truly personal nature was found.

It was worth bearing in mind.

On the way out he met Lucy Lane, newly arrived with DCs Curnow and Potter.

Detective Sergeant Lucy Lane, thirtyish, now an experienced member of the squad, had surmounted the hazards of being both female and attractive in a hand-picked brotherhood. A caustic and ready wit had been more than equal to the Romeo element, but the male chauvinists had proved more refractory.

'Mr Kersey expects to come down this afternoon or first thing in the morning unless you tell him to the contrary.'

'Good! I want you, Lucy, to concentrate on finding out about Miller's friends and associates; who he mixed with, either on the estate or in the village. Did he have people staying here? Find out what the village thought of him. Get your DCs taking the routine statements from the principals and muster what help Reed can give for a clip-board exercise. We want gossip. I'm going to quiz his lordship on Miller's background.'

It was classic procedure: first get to know the victim; once you do, the chances are that you will discover why he became one. You might even find out who made him one.

He was less conscious of location now, more absorbed in the routine of a murder inquiry which is much the same anywhere. He arranged for an Incident Van to be positioned in the open space near the estate entrance.

As he was passing in front of the big house he encountered the vanguard of the press – two of them, not conspicuously fired by a great sense of mission. There had been a brief press release from headquarters the previous afternoon, scarcely noticed by the media: 'A thirty-seven-year-old man, Mr Anthony Miller, was found shot dead in his cottage on the Duloe Estate this morning. When found, the dead man was seated in a chair with his shotgun between his knees. Mr Miller was employed as foreman on the estate and he lived alone. The circumstances of his death are being investigated.'

As a news item it had all the drama of the classic: 'Small earthquake in Chile; few casualties.'

Now interest was building; no doubt spies had reported a take-over by crime squad.

'Is this a murder investigation, Mr Wycliffe?'

'So it seems.'

'Dressed up as suicide?'

'The situation was as described in the press release.'

'Do you have any idea of why Miller was shot or who was responsible?'

'At the moment I have no idea.'

The questions continued but the answers were no more profitable and at length Wycliffe escaped to go in search of Lord Bottrell. Instead of going up to the front door he went around to the back, acting on the principle that the back of a building is usually more informative than the front. It is where they keep the plumbing.

He passed under a broad granite arch into a large paved yard with the house forming one side and outbuildings the other three. A section of the yard had been walled off to form the court with its ash tree. Everywhere there were signs of neglect and decay. Grass grew between the cobbles and there were places where the cobbles had been dug up and not replaced. The back of the house itself was in fairly good trim, but for the outbuildings the story was one of peeling paintwork, crumbling mortar, and loose or missing slates.

Much of the former coach house was now no more than an open shed housing several motor vehicles, but the remainder had been turned into an estate office. There was a sign saying so: 'Duloe Estate Office. All enquiries'. As well start there as anywhere; he was, after all, on what Perry Mason used to call a 'fishing trip'.

A young woman, hammering away at a typewriter, paused to ask him his business, then: 'Lord Bottrell is in his office – through there.'

Informality was clearly the order of the day.

He was received with something very like warmth and wondered how long it would last.

'I don't employ an agent – can't afford one – so I have to do the work myself. Lander does the clever bits, he's got the know-how and the staff. He has a large practice in Truro but he always finds time for our troubles.'

The office was plain, sparsely furnished, but businesslike: a desk, filing cabinets, a set of drawers for plans, bookshelves with books on the law and estate management and, on one wall, a large-scale map showed the estate lands outlined in red. Hung in a place of honour, over the fireplace, was a rather romanticized watercolour of the house seen from the river.

Bottrell said: 'John Varley in the eighteen-thirties. Not especially valuable but I'm very fond of it . . .'

Wycliffe was more interested in the map. The house and its outbuildings were shown in considerable detail and, at some distance, nearer to the upper of the two creeks than he had supposed, was Treave. Midway between the two houses Miller's cottage was shown close to a footpath through the wood. Wycliffe noticed a second isolated little building, on the creekside, below Treave.

'Is that a house?'

Bottrell came to stand beside him. 'Tytreth – Cornish for ferry house because there was once a ferry across the creek there. It's on Treave property, not mine. Until a couple of years ago an old couple lived there but they moved into sheltered accommodation in Truro and since then Lander has fitted it out for his photography. He's a photography buff – quite well known; he writes articles and things . . . Anyway, I don't suppose that is what you came to talk about.'

'No. I want to get as complete a picture as possible of the dead man, the kind of life he led, and the people with whom he was most closely associated.' Wycliffe added, with apparent casualness: 'All we have at the moment is a few fingerprints.'

Bottrell was quick to respond: 'Mine amongst them, I expect.'

'Perhaps; it would help if we could make a comparison – for elimination purposes.'

'Of course! Send along your chap with his little inky pad any time.'

'Thank you. Now, returning to Miller, what can you tell me about his family, his background, his life before he came here?'

'Very little; he was not very communicative. I know hardly more now than I did five years ago when he took the job.'

'Presumably there was a written application and references?'

Bottrell went to one of the filing cabinets and returned with a file containing only three or four sheets of paper. 'This is it.' He spread the papers on his desk. 'Born and educated at Church Stretton, Shropshire . . . Did pretty well at school – O-levels, A-levels . . . And after all that, a job in a local garage . . . Maintenance man at a horticultural college . . . Ditto at a country park in Lancashire . . .'

'Gaps?'

Bottrell glanced through the papers. 'There could have been, I suppose; this isn't overloaded with dates.'

'References?'

'Copies of testimonials from his employers enclosed with the application.'

'You didn't take up references?'

'The money wasn't attractive; there were six applications of which his was the only one remotely suitable so I had him down, liked what I saw, and appointed him.'

'Perhaps I could borrow that file. What other employees have you, sir?'

A wry smile. 'Very few. Outside, apart from Tony, only Harry Biddick, the gardener; he lives close by, on the road to the village. Then there's Delia, my secretary; she's from the village.'

'You run this place with two men?'

'I wish I could. No, I employ casual labour and contractors as I need them – it's cheaper. Tony's job was to keep an eye on that side – mostly the farms; they are let to tenants but I'm responsible for repairs.'

'And in the house?'

'No retinue of servants there either, I'm afraid; a man and his wife – Ralph and Jill Christophers – living in, and a couple of girls from the village, part-time. For a while we had a girl living in but she left and I don't think we shall replace her.'

'So, actually living on the estate, apart from you, Lady Bottrell, and your son, there are three people: Dr James Bottrell, and the Christophers, man and wife. Your gardener, your secretary, and two maids, live out. You realize that we may have to interview these people?'

'Of course.'

The smooth tanned features were composed. He waited for any further questions, tolerant and relaxed. In their previous encounter his wife had been a disturbing influence.

'It seems that he had homosexual companions; do you know who they were?'

A vague gesture. 'He was a free agent, the house was his to do as he liked as long as he worked here.'

'It seems there was also a woman who was at least a frequent visitor.'

'Really? Isn't it the case that some men are bisexual?' A quick smile. 'You should talk to James about it, he's an expert on abnormal psychology.'

'You've no idea who this woman might have been?'

'None.'

'I understand from Lander that he had visitors at the cottage from time to time.'

'Lander would probably know.'

'You were there fairly often – would you say every day?'

A sharp look, prompted by this first direct, personal question, but Wycliffe's manner was bland, his expression mild, anything but threatening.

'I suppose I called in at the cottage most days.'

'But you saw no-one there other than Miller?'

'Of course he was not always alone.'

'Did you ever see a woman there?'

Bottrell was becoming slightly flustered. 'Once or twice, I think. I didn't take a lot of notice.' He gathered his wits. 'You must understand, Mr Wycliffe, that when I arrived any visitor would realize I wanted to talk business with Miller and generally they would leave us to get on with it.'

'I see.' Perhaps the most non-committal phrase in the language and enough to leave Bottrell with a vague disquiet.

'When was the last time you saw him alive?'

A frown. 'Saturday evening – the day after he returned from his holiday.'

'Can you put a time to your visit?'

'It wasn't a visit; I happened to meet him in South Wood when I was out for a stroll, about seven it must have been. Tony was often out around that time – usually with his gun; he liked to shoot the odd rabbit or a brace of pigeons for the pot – he was a good cook.'

'Did he have his gun on that occasion?'

'No.'

'Did he seem his usual self?'

Bottrell hesitated. 'As I told you he came back early from his holiday. It was obvious that something was preying on his mind but I've no idea what. When I met him on Saturday evening he was withdrawn, inclined to be sullen . . .'

'Do you do any shooting, Lord Bottrell?'

'No. It doesn't appeal to me. My brother does a bit – he occasionally borrows Tony's gun, but as a family we don't live up to the country tradition, I'm afraid.'

'It seems that he spent at least part of his holiday in Dorchester; does that mean anything to you?'

'Dorchester? No, not a thing.'

Wycliffe got up from his chair. 'Well, thank you, sir. I shan't trouble you any more for the moment.'

He was escorted through the outer office to the yard where Bottrell made conversation for a minute or two, then: 'You must come in for drinks one evening. Cynthia would like that.'

On the point of leaving, Wycliffe turned back. 'Just one more thing, sir. I wonder if you can tell me who owns the vehicles in the garage over there?'

'But of course! The Rover is mine and the Mini belongs to Cynthia. James lays claim to the old Vauxhall, and the Escort hatchback was Tony's. The Land Rover is a general workhorse for the estate.'

'Did Miller take his car on holiday?'

'He certainly took it but he could have left it in the station car park at Truro and carried on by train. That is what I do whenever I go anywhere at a distance.'

'When did he leave?'

Bottrell considered. 'Monday – a week ago yesterday. He must have set out early – before eight; he was already gone when I made my rounds as I do every morning before breakfast.'

Wycliffe thanked him again and left. Despite his apparent candour his lordship was hiding something – quite a lot, Wycliffe thought. The question was whether he was hiding anything relevant. In any case no point in a frontal assault now, better to wait for the ammunition train.

Half-past twelve; Wycliffe went to lunch at the pub where he was staying, pleased to slip into a new routine. Whenever he was forced to break a regular habit he was uncomfortable until he had formed a new one.

There were several men around the bar and one of them, a wizened little fellow wearing a black peaked cap, was holding forth oratorically. He broke off as he caught sight of Wycliffe. There were free tables in the adjoining dining area and Wycliffe went through. The blackboard read: 'Dish of the day: Home-made Cottage Pie'.

He chose a table in an alcove. Helen had once accused him of living in a psychological alcove, wanting to see without being seen. It was true that he hated being up front, on view.

'A menu, sir?' A plump girl who had been serving in the bar the night before.

'No, I'll take the dish of the day . . . and a glass of dry white wine.'

The waitress brought his wine and he sipped it while waiting. He was trying to make some sort of pattern out of what he had learned since arriving at Duloe. The central character was the dead man; a homosexual living alone in a remote cottage. Witnesses agreed that he had been depressed when he returned from his holiday and it seemed that the killer had tried to take advantage of this by rigging a fake suicide.

So far his thoughts were clear, but beyond that point logical reasoning failed him as it often did. He was left with a rag-bag of phrases and images which cropped up in his mind unbidden and in no particular sequence.

'At least with closed eyes – isn't that essential to being harmless?' Lord Bottrell on the family totem.

' . . . gay and inclined to be promiscuous.' Lady Bottrell.

'I fancy she's more mother than mistress to our Hugh.' Dr Franks. And Franks again: 'Sometimes I get the impression that Lander works him by strings.'

' . . . gays who are unfaithful to their lovers run a greater risk of a jealous revenge . . .' Beth Lander.

'You should talk to James, he's an expert on abnormal psychology.' Lord Bottrell.

His pie arrived, an individual one in its own dish. With his fork he probed the nicely browned potato topping and found plenty of meat in a rich gravy underneath.

'Mind if I join you, sir?' It was the little man in the black cap – which he kept on.

Wycliffe did mind, there were other tables, but he had been well brought up, taught to wash behind his ears, not to pick his nose, and to be polite to strangers: 'Not at all.'

'I could do you a bit of good.'

Wycliffe began eating and said nothing.

'I'm Bottrell's father-in-law.'

Still no response.

'What's that you're drinking?'

'White wine.'

'I'd rather have a whisky.'

'You've just come from the bar.'

'What I've got to tell you, Mister, is worth more than a bloody whisky. For starters, my daughter's husband – his lordship, is a poof.'

'What is your name?'

'Me? I'm Ernie Sims; like I told you my daughter is married to—'

'Well, Mr Sims, if you have anything to tell the police in connection with the death of Anthony Miller you should go to the Incident Van at the entrance to Duloe and make a statement.'

'Like hell! The reporters will listen to me.'

'I expect they will but I doubt if they'll pay because they won't be stupid enough to print what you tell them.' Wycliffe wished that were true. 'Now, perhaps you will let me get on with my meal. If you do not attend at the Incident Van I may send an officer to interview you at your home.'

'Are you threatening me?'

'If you choose to think so.'

The little man got up, muttered something, and went back to the bar.

Wycliffe was intrigued. He wondered what manner of woman who, with this unpromising assistance, had contrived to produce Lady Bottrell. There was more to it than the luck of the genetic bran tub, there was upbringing. No wonder the poor woman, after marrying off her daughter, had given up the unequal struggle, and died.

As he was leaving, three men came in. Wycliffe recognized two of them as agency reporters. They saw him and grinned with amiable camaraderie. Lord Bottrell's father-in-law was set fair to get drunk.

Chapter Five

The Incident Van – a king-sized caravan – was in position near the entrance to the estate. Under the blind eyes of the recumbent cats a uniformed policeman patrolled, ready to repel boarders or at least to check visitors. The van would provide a local base and communications centre for officers on the case. There were a couple of typewriters with VDU screens for their use though the bulk of the recording would still be done at sub-division. DS Shaw, Wycliffe's administrative assistant, was organizing that end.

Lucy Lane was already installed in the van. DCs Curnow and Potter were taking statements from the principals, while Reed's men were on house-to-house enquiries: 'How well did you know the dead man? . . . When did you last see him? . . . Can you tell us anything about his way of life, his friends, or anything else that might assist our enquiries? Where were you on Sunday night? . . . Did you, at any time, hear a shot?'

The mills of God were trundling into action.

The van was new and Wycliffe wandered through the compartments looking at this and that. At one end there was a little cubbyhole for the officer in charge. He came back to stand by Lucy's chair and said, musing: 'He must have done something.'

'Sir?'

'Miller – must have done something to get himself killed.'

It was not a very profound statement, coming from the head of CID, yet it expressed quite simply his belief that in most murder cases the victim is an active participant in his own death. There is something he has done, or heard, or seen, or known . . .

'I want this fingerprint business sorted out, Lucy. Lord Bottrell has volunteered. Send somebody with a bit of tact; I don't want Fox upsetting the customers. As cover, if for no other reason, we shall need to do his brother and Lander also. Send Curnow, he knows how to keep his big feet out of things.'

He was staring out of the window and thinking that of all the places where he had worked from a van this was probably the strangest. The high, almost circular wall, forming a sort of amphitheatre, the stone pillars with their emblematic cats, the trees – these things together with that sense of isolation, created an impression of some archaeological site which had remained undisturbed for centuries.

'And another thing, Lucy: get in touch with Dorset CID. Miller stayed at the Crown in Dorchester for the four nights of his holiday. We shall be grateful for anything they can get; in particular whether he arrived by car, whether he had a companion, how he spent his time . . . It's only a few days ago. We could be lucky.'

So Lord Bottrell was homosexual. That was no surprise; he had suspected as much on sight, and her ladyship had dropped hints. So what? Homosexuality was not invented by Wolfenden, nor was it ever confined to communities of one sex. Look at the chronicles of Bloomsbury.

What mattered was that everything pointed to Bottrell having been involved with the dead man, and if Bottrell and Miller were lovers . . . With her talk of homosexual jealousy Beth Lander had deliberately seeded an idea she had wanted him to have. Why?

Well, Bottrell would have to come clean and Wycliffe suspected that he would make a virtue out of necessity. But there was much more to it than that; he was a long way from any hint of a pattern.

He had reached the door of the van when Lucy called to him. 'Where will you be if . . . ?'

'Out.'

He walked down the drive, past the house and on down the sloping parkland towards the river. The sheep eyed him without interrupting their grazing. He passed through the screen of trees and found himself on a quay largely overgrown with brambles and gorse with a few spindly sycamores. It was about half-tide; the river was smooth, bottle-green near the shore, catching the sun further out. The numerous bends shut out any distant prospect, creating the illusion of a landlocked water. Not a soul anywhere. Then an eldritch screech echoed across the valley, a heron taking off from the opposite bank. It flew low across the water and landed not far away to merge at once with the background. And he was in this place to investigate a murder.

A little to his right, he caught sight of a low roof almost hidden by shrubs. He walked towards it along a well worn path. It was a boathouse with walls of hand-sawn planks, grey-green with lichen, and a roof of rough-hewn slate. Some of the planks were rotten and there were slates missing from the roof. Old buildings are like old people, they can be ripe and mellow or ignoble and depressing. The boathouse had reached that point when one wished that it could be frozen in time. A door in the side was open and he went in.

A fine old place; a wet dock surrounded on three sides by a wooden platform, all under cover. In the dock there were two craft; a rowing skiff and a rather splendid launch with plenty of varnished wood and brasswork, now tarnished. She had a cabin amidships and *MV Jezebel* on her transom.

Despite the end open to the river, wooded banks and dark water combined to produce a church-like gloom in the boathouse and slight movements of the water outside caused a rhythmic chuckling under the duck boards.

As his eyes became accustomed to the dim light he saw that there was another door in the far end. It was partly open and he could see into some sort of storeroom. He decided to take a closer look but as he approached, the door opened wide and Jean Lander came out.

'I thought I heard somebody,' she said. A slight figure, her burnished red hair was about her shoulders and by contrast her face seemed unnaturally pale. She was dressed as he had last seen her, in the uniform of the young: T-shirt and jeans, now with trainers added. She stood, expectant, on the edge of defiance.

He tried to disarm her. 'Isn't this a splendid boathouse!'

She looked about her without interest. 'Yes, I suppose it is. I think it's the only one left on the river.'

'Do you go boating with the Bottrells?'

'I used to but they don't take Jezebel out now. Lord Bottrell prefers sailing and he keeps a boat down river at Restronguet.'

She remained tense, prepared to make polite conversation but waiting for what she knew must come.

He said: 'You lied to me last night, Jean, and that means you lied in your statement.'

'Yes.'

'I don't know why or how you lied, only that you are not very good at it.'

Her eyes were dark-ringed. For a while she said

nothing. He wondered what she had been doing in the boathouse. He could see into the room from which she had come: all sorts of gear was stored against the walls and on the floor: oars, coiled ropes, a couple of kedge anchors, an outboard motor, oil drums . . . It all looked as though it had remained undisturbed for a long time.

'Are you going to tell me about it?'

When she spoke her tone was flat, matter-of-fact: 'What I said about finding Tony Miller was untrue. It was during the night that we found him.'

'We?'

'Paul was with me – Paul Bottrell.' She took a deep breath. 'On Sunday night we went out after my parents thought I was in bed.' She added after a pause, defensive: 'We don't do that sort of thing often; Sunday was only the second time.'

'When was the first?'

'The Sunday before.'

'Any particular reason for choosing Sundays?'

She flushed. 'It's just that my father usually spends the night at his studio on Sundays – where he does his photography.'

'You came here?'

'Yes, we took the skiff and went for a row.'

'Couldn't you do that in the day?' It sounded like the silly question it was.

She frowned. 'It was more fun to meet at night. In any case my father doesn't like me being with Paul; he doesn't like me having boyfriends.'

'So what happened on Sunday night?'

She brushed her hair back from her eyes with a girlish gesture, a trick which owed all to genes and nothing to guile but Wycliffe was moved. Sex had entered the equation. Policeman and judges are not neutered; perhaps they should be.

She said: 'Well, when we came back and we'd put the skiff away Paul was taking me home by the short cut through the spinney—'

'What time was this?'

'About half-past one in the morning, perhaps a bit later. There was a light in Tony's living-room and his front door was wide open. Earlier, just before twelve, when we passed the cottage his door was shut and he was playing the flute. That was nothing unusual; Tony was known for staying up half the night, but when we came back a lot later and found his door open . . . Anyway, Paul went in to see if he was all right.

'Of course, he was dead.' She let the words fall with bleak finality.

'And you told no-one.'

'We knew that he was dead, we thought he had killed himself, and there was nothing anybody could do.'

'Did you see him?'

She nodded and turned away.

'You realize that you and Paul between you may well have made the catching of a killer more difficult. You not only withheld information but you made a false statement to the police.'

She flushed and her lips were trembling so that he thought she might burst into tears, but after an interval she spoke in a low voice: 'It was my fault; I know it was a terrible thing to do but I was scared of my father. I thought somebody was bound to find Tony in the morning and that a few hours couldn't make any difference.'

'But despite all that you pretended to find him yourself.'

She nodded. 'I couldn't sleep and when it was morning, with people moving about again and still no news, I couldn't stand it any longer; I had to do something . . .'

'Did you tell Paul?'

'Yes, she did, but afterwards.'

They had not heard him approach. Paul was standing in the doorway, a lean silhouette, his manner, even his posture was nervous, tentative, yet aggressive.

Wycliffe ignored him. 'What about your father? What does he know about all this?'

She said: 'He knew that I was out with Paul Sunday night. I don't know how he found out. He didn't say anything that morning but in the evening, before you came, he had me in his room.'

'He was angry?'

She nodded.

'Does he know that you found Miller's body while you were out?'

'I don't think so.'

'You don't know?'

She made a curious little movement as though defending herself. 'I can't tell with Father . . . He saves things up.'

The boy said: 'You've no idea what it's like. He hits her.'

'Stop it, Paul!'

Wycliffe turned to the boy. 'It was definitely you who discovered the body? You may have to swear to it in court.'

He was surly. 'Yes, Jean stayed outside at first.'

'When you passed the cottage earlier, and heard the flute, did you form any impression that Miller had company?'

'No.'

Jean said: 'He only played when he was alone.'

'Let him answer. Between then and when you returned to find him dead, did you hear anything else?'

'You mean the shot?'

'You heard a shot?'

'Yes, but we didn't take much notice. You occasionally do hear a shot at night; somebody after a fox or somebody trying to poach old Roskilly's deer – he rears them for venison and poachers have had one or two goes.'

'How long was it after you heard the shot before you got back to the cottage?'

'We were in the boat when we heard it; it must have been a good hour.'

'Where, exactly, were you?'

'On the river, about a couple of hundred yards upstream from here.'

'Can you show me from the shore?'

The girl said: 'I suppose so.'

They led the way back to the overgrown quay, crossed it, and followed a narrow path along the river bank, walking in single file.

Paul said: 'This path runs along the shore of the creek, more or less; in fact you can get to the village this way if you don't mind a bit of mud.'

'Past Mr Lander's studio?'

The girl turned her head to look back at him. 'Yes, it does, but that's a good way on.' Her manner was curt. 'Anyway you can see where we were from here.'

They were on a beach. Shrubs and a few trees, their roots largely exposed in the crumbling bank, fringed a stretch of muddy shingle which was probably covered at the top of the tide.

Jean pointed. 'We were there, just at the entrance to the creek, in the channel.'

'And, according to you, it must have been about half-past twelve.'

It was Paul who answered: 'That's as near as I can get.'

Wycliffe said: 'All this happened the night before last but you've kept it to yourselves until now.'

They were silent. Wycliffe saw someone standing, watching them from up the slope, among the trees; a young man, stockily built, dressed in jeans and a bomber jacket. 'Who's that?'

Paul followed his gaze. 'Matt Biddick; his father works on the estate. He's dotty about birds and all kinds of wild life. He's always around when he isn't working.'

'What does he do?'

'Pretty well anything. Whenever anybody is short handed they send for Matt.'

'Going back to Sunday night; is there anything else you haven't chosen to tell me?'

They were silent for a while then Jean said: 'There is something. While Paul was in the cottage I saw somebody.'

'Go on.'

'I was waiting at the edge of the clearing and I saw somebody at the side of the cottage – to the left when you face the front. He was only there for a moment. I think he saw me in the light from the front door and drew back. I've no idea who it was.'

'But it was a man?'

'I thought so. There was just once when I caught sight of his face but it was only a sort of blur.'

'What did you do?'

'Well, I was a bit scared and I ran across to the cottage. That was when I went in . . .' Her voice trailed off.

The boy said: 'When we came out Jean told me about the man and we looked, but we couldn't find anybody.'

Wycliffe let out a deep sigh: 'Of course you will both have to make full statements setting out all this. Neither of you comes out of it with any credit.'

A motor boat with a family party aboard putt-putted downstream and for a minute or two the odd little group on the shingle was the centre of their attention.

When they had disappeared round the next bend the boy said, 'There's something I wanted to ask . . .' His grey eyes sought Wycliffe's in concern. 'Is it true that when the police came there was a string tied to the trigger of the shotgun?'

'Yes.'

'Well, I don't think there was when I saw it. I know I was upset but I remember wondering how he could have reached the trigger . . .'

Wycliffe stooped, picked up one of the flat stones and tried to send it skimming across the water. It bounced once, and sank. He said: 'I'm no good at it.'

Not surprisingly, the pair looked at him, uncomprehending.

When they had left, Wycliffe set out along the path which led eventually to the village. Probably at almost any other time he would have had to pick his way through squelchy mud but three weeks of drought and sunshine had baked the surface of the path to a brick-like hardness.

He reached the creek; it was broad at first but narrowed to vanishing point in the middle distance where the tower of the village church rose out of the trees. Opposite him, on the other bank, there were fields of corn ready for cutting, there were houses strung out along the shore, and a jetty with a veritable flotilla of small craft moored off. But on his side he could see nothing but thinly wooded slopes and the path pursuing a sinuous course along the edge of the tidal mud. Lander's studio must be tucked away, around a corner.

He had learned something from the two youngsters: the shot which killed Miller had been fired at 12.30; a nice round fact to put on paper. But he had learned too of complications: the Lander girl had seen a man at the side of the cottage an hour later. It would make sense to suppose that he had been inside when young Bottrell went to investigate, that he was the killer, and that he had escaped by the back door only to find his escape temporarily blocked by the girl.

He strolled comfortably, missing only the consolation of his pipe; a year or so of voluntary deprivation had not altogether quelled the pangs of addiction. Thoughts drifted across his mind, inconsequential and tenuous. How often had he wished that he could think as he supposed others did? A is to B as C is to D so XYZ must follow. But did anybody really think like that?

Back to the man Jean Lander had seen: what was he doing, lurking around the cottage an hour after the killing? Faking the suicide? It was possible. Why had it taken so long? And there was the boy's story of the string, and Fox's suspicion about an earlier search. Had the man returned?

He thought of the young couple: an odd pair thrown together as refugees from their parents. They had withheld information and the girl had made a false statement; he should have breathed fire but he hadn't – and wouldn't.

The path rounded a promontory at the entrance to the upper creek. Here the foreshore was rocky, and above the tide mark, there were indications of former industry: a roofless stone building, its walls covered with ivy; vestiges of a slipway; and baulks of timber, blackened by age, set upright in the ground. Here and there channels had been cut into the rock for some purpose now obscure.

Nestling in the angle of the promontory was Tytreth – Lander's studio, a grim little building of slatey stone with granite coigns and a slate roof. It was built into the slope of the hill well clear of the tide and backed by trees. A paved slipway of weedy granite setts ran down to the water.

A convoy of mute swans cruised past in formation, now and then dipping their necks to scavenge the bottom mud; otherwise there was no movement anywhere, and no sound. Despite the picture-postcard houses across the creek, the moored boats, and the church tower upstream, it was easy to imagine that this was a countryside recently evacuated in the face of some sudden and mysterious scourge. The cottage helped the illusion: the windows were shuttered on the inside, the door was an affair of massive planks secured by a hefty padlock, and above the door was a little grey box bearing the words: 'Securex Alarm System'.

Looking up through the trees, above and behind the cottage, Wycliffe could make out a gable and a window belonging to Treave House. Was Lander defending this outpost against raiders by sea?

He opened a narrow, iron gate labelled 'Private' and climbed some steps beside the cottage. They brought him to a well-kept but steep path through the trees and a minute or two later he was in Lander's drive, not far from the white gate. Instead of letting himself out by the gate he took the path through the spinney which would take him past Miller's cottage.

It troubled him sometimes that his actions seemed almost as inconsequential as his thoughts. What had prompted this meandering exploration which had taken up a good deal of his afternoon? What would he do now? No-one could accuse him of being hamstrung by some preconceived idea or plan. Sometimes he felt like a small boy with a jigsaw puzzle, picking out the bits which attracted him because of their pretty colours or interesting shapes. If someone had pressed him to justify his whimsical procedures he would probably have muttered:

'I don't know if I can; I call it field work.'

It was as he emerged from the trees in front of the big house that he decided he was on his way to talk to his lordship's brother, the psychologist.

'He has a sort of lair in the old stables . . .' Lady Bottrell, on her brother-in-law.

The stable yard opened off the main yard. Smaller, and cobbled like the other, some attempt had been made to preserve it; the cobbles were free of weeds, the walls had been freshly pointed, and the stone drinking trough in the middle was now an ornamental feature. Much of the former stable building had been demolished, leaving only the foundations, but the end with a loft had been converted into an attractive little house, startling in its incongruity.

The varnished door was not quite shut and from inside he could hear the rattle of a typewriter. There was no bell or knocker so he rapped with his knuckles.

'Come in!' A peremptory command.

After the sunlight the room seemed to be in darkness but as his eyes accommodated he saw James Bottrell, seated at a long table, doing a rapid two-finger exercise on an old Remington. The table was littered from end to end with books, pocket files, and heaps of loose papers. The wall spaces were taken up with bookshelves and row upon row of box files.

It was a strange room, long and narrow and high, like the nave of a church. At one end a spiral iron staircase led up to a gallery from which other rooms opened off. Daylight came from a skylight over the gallery and from a high window at the other end.

'So you've found me; now find yourself a seat.' Bottrell typed to the end of a page, ripped out paper and carbons from the machine and separated them. 'Be with you in a minute . . . There!'

Wycliffe had found a seat. Bottrell removed his spectacles and regarded him across the table. 'I suppose this is about Miller.'

'How well did you know him?'

'I knew him; it was through me that he got the job here.'

'Really? Your brother didn't mention that.'

'He doesn't know. He was advertising for a foreman; it was the sort of job Miller wanted at the time so I suggested he should apply. If Hugh had known I had a hand in it Miller wouldn't have stood a chance.' The grey eyes were steady, as though challenging a response.

'How did you—'

Bottrell cut him short. 'It must have been early in '84. At that time I was a consultant in the North Midlands and Miller was referred to me.'

'What was his problem?'

Bottrell shrugged. 'He was sexually insecure. A man with strong homosexual compulsions accompanied by guilt. His GP sensibly decided that a stitch in time might save him from your lot and the barred windows.'

'He had committed an offence?'

'Perhaps, but if he had, nobody had preferred charges. Anyway, I thought a course of rural quietude the best prescription, so I put him in the way of applying for Hugh's job.'

He paused to take a cigarette from a box, and light it. He pushed the box across the table to Wycliffe. 'Smoke?'

'No, thanks.'

'Given it up.' It was a statement, not a question.

'I used to smoke a pipe.'

The grey eyes regarded him, thoughtful and unblinking, so that he felt like a specimen. Finally, Bottrell said: 'One of those who prefers the world he knows to oblivion or a dubious alternative.'

Wycliffe felt the need to assert himself. 'You saw a good deal of Miller?'

'He came here to play chess once or twice a week. He was good.'

'Did you go to his cottage?'

'Hardly ever.'

'I've been told that Miller was promiscuous.'

Bottrell let the ash from his cigarette drop on to his shirt and brushed it away with an irritable movement. 'My sister-in-law wanted to believe it, at least to convince Hugh that it was so.'

'Why would she wish to do that?'

Bottrell looked at him for a moment then said: 'You don't need me to spell it out.'

Wycliffe was scanning the labels on one shelf of box files: Community Factors, Social Group, Genetic Factors, Family Background, Political Allegiance, Race . . .

Bottrell said: 'Clumsy, isn't it? I should have started with a computer; now it would be too much of a bind, transferring all that on to disc or tape. But it's frustrating, working near the end of the century with equipment appropriate to the thirties.' He waved his cigarette in a broad gesture. 'Do you realize, Wycliffe, that we've arrived at another *fin de siècle*? And the last one was the prelude to 1914. The issues are different but the menace is greater: this "disease called man" has now reached epidemic proportions.' His lips twisted in an odd little grin. 'Yet you've given up smoking so, presumably, you want to stay on to see the fun.'

Wycliffe was trying to find a footing with this man who looked like a slow witted bear but had a quick-silver mind.

'When did you last see Miller?'

'Sunday evening.'

'Any idea of the time?'

Bottrell inhaled on his cigarette and blew out a cloud of grey smoke. 'Between nine and ten. I was here working when he walked in.'

'You may well have been the last person to see him alive other than his killer. Did he seem distressed, excited, depressed?'

'You're asking me did I see him as a man likely to commit suicide or get himself murdered within the next couple of hours. The answer is no, he wasn't much different to usual, a bit more taciturn perhaps.'

'What did he want?'

An amused glance. 'What do people want from the chap next door? If they're not borrowing the lawn mower or come to complain about the dog, it's human contact, and not necessarily to talk. I asked him if he'd like a game of chess but he refused. He sat where you are for about fifteen minutes; he didn't say much – a few banal remarks. I had the impression he was trying to make up his mind whether he wanted to talk or not.'

'He was troubled?'

'He had something on his mind but I've no idea what.'

'Something which happened while he was away, perhaps?'

'Perhaps.'

'Whoever killed him played up the idea of depression in rigging an apparent suicide.'

'Then he or she was a poor psychologist. If there is such a thing as a suicidal type, Miller was not one. What's more, the fact that your chap spotted the fake so readily suggests that the killer wasn't very bright.'

'A poor psychologist and not very bright. You haven't greatly narrowed my field.'

Bottrell grinned. 'Pity! Most cops I come across are bastards but you don't seem a bad sort.'

'One more thing: we think there was a woman at the cottage, either as a frequent visitor or perhaps living there for a time.'

'That wouldn't surprise me.'

'Despite his homosexuality?'

A wry smile. 'Kinsey should be required reading for coppers, Mr Wycliffe. There are all degrees of homosexuality; attitudes and behaviour patterns are as varied as with heterosexuals. Even the committed male homosexual may be painfully aware of his deviance from the accepted norm. He may feel that by establishing a relationship with a woman he will be able to resist his homosexual drive and perhaps overcome it. It rarely works.'

'Have you any idea who this woman at the cottage could have been?'

Bottrell seemed to hesitate. 'The only woman who's been around and isn't now is Lizzie Biddick. She was a maid at the house – living in.'

'What happened to her?'

'She left. I can't say exactly when but it was very recent. You could ask Cynthia.'

'A local girl?'

'Her father, Harry Biddick, is Hugh's gardener.'

'And Matt Biddick, the birdwatcher, is her brother?'

Bottrell grinned. 'You're learning. There's a whole tribe of them; they live just up the road, towards the village.'

There was an interval while Wycliffe tried to bring about an awkward silence – one which the other party feels driven to break. It didn't work with Bottrell; he sat relaxed, complacent, and waited. A little battery clock on the table clicked away more than a minute and it was Wycliffe who spoke first.

'I've just come from Lander's studio.'

'Really? An escorted visit?'

'No. I walked round by the shore out of curiosity. The place is like Fort Knox.'

'Lander's photographic hide-out. He keeps his collection there and a lot of expensive equipment.'

'His collection?'

'Photographs of historical interest. You should get him to show you; I believe they're quite valuable.'

'Do you see much of the Landers?'

'Not more than I can help. Lander is a solemn ass and his wife is a harridan. She pretends to be a victim of marriage but it's Lander who's the victim and he's too big a fool to see it. I think you've met their girl – Jean; she drops in here occasionally.'

'For?'

'God knows! She drifts in here, looks things over with that detached insolence of the young girl learning to be a woman. She asks odd questions about anything that happens to be on her mind at the moment, then drifts out again. Still, I prefer them at that age to what they become later.'

'You don't like women, Dr Bottrell?'

Bottrell laughed. 'God's second mistake, Nietzsche called them; but I find them necessary, and sometimes amusing.'

Wycliffe was running out of questions but, like a dog worrying a bone, he was reluctant to give up.

'After Miller left you on Sunday evening, what did you do?'

Bottrell frowned. 'As far as I remember I read for a while then went to bed.'

'You were alone?'

'Unfortunately, I usually am.'

'You did not hear a shot?'

'When I sleep, I sleep.'

Wycliffe stood up. 'Thanks; I've no doubt we shall meet again.'

Bottrell limped after him to the door. 'Do you play chess?'

'Not on duty.'

'Pity! With Miller gone I'm reduced to intellectual masturbation.'

'Damn the man!' Wycliffe was back in the big yard behind the house, sore with himself rather than Bottrell. He felt outclassed; he had allowed Bottrell to make the running and all because he had ignored the first commandment in the holy writ of interviewing technique: 'Always assume that the other party is at least as intelligent and quick witted as you are.' All the same he had learned something, though, he suspected, only those things which Bottrell had wanted him to know. In fact there had been an element of forced feeding.

He decided to look for a quicker way to the cottage than trotting around three sides of the house. He found it in a small arched entrance to a kitchen yard where there were dustbins and a clothes hoist. A second arch opened on the east side and through it he could see the spinney within a hundred yards. As he passed under the first arch a woman came to stand in the doorway of what, presumably, was the kitchen.

'Can I help you, sir?'

'You are Mrs Christophers?'

She smiled. 'And you must be the police gentleman.'

A contradiction in terms? He hoped not. She was younger than he had expected – thirty-five? On the plump side though not fat, a mass of brown hair, a clear skin, and dark brown eyes – no Celt, but Cornish through and through. Why the real Cornish pretend to be Celts nobody will ever know; or the Bretons, or the

Welsh, or the Irish. Why not leave it to the brawny, bony, sandy-haired Scots in whom Julius Caesar would certainly recognize his old enemies.

'Lord Bottrell told us about you.'

'I would like a word . . . Chief Superintendent Wycliffe.'

'You best come in, then.' She held out a soft hand. 'Jill Christophers. Pleased to meet you, I'm sure.'

The kitchen was large with plenty of unused space because modern appliances and utensils take up so little room. The floor was carpeted and every working surface shone.

'I was just making a pot of tea, if you'd like a cup, Mr Wycliffe. My Ralph will be here any minute; that man can smell the teapot a mile off.' She laughed.

And she was right; almost at once her husband arrived with an assortment of vegetables in a basket. 'Harry says there's no runner beans worth picking today, they'll have to have carrots as a second veg tonight.' He caught sight of the intruder. 'Oh, I didn't know . . . Mr Wycliffe, is that right? . . . Ralph Christophers.'

'You like it strong? . . . Do sit down for goodness sake!'

'Strongish,' Wycliffe said. 'A little milk but no sugar, please.'

'Might almost be a Cornishman. Now then, Ralph, Mr Wycliffe wants to ask us a few questions.'

Ralph Christophers was small and spare, about the same age as his wife but without her ebullient cheerfulness. He sat in what was obviously 'his place' and looked at Wycliffe with a sombre air. 'I don't want you to misunderstand me, Mr Wycliffe, but Jill and me work here – we're employed, and it begins and ends there. That seems to us the best way.'

'And that wasn't true of Tony Miller?'

Christophers sipped his tea and looked at Wycliffe over the cup. 'Well he was employed too but he was a different class and he was on terms with his lordship that you might call friendly.'

Jill nodded. 'That's right.'

'So?'

'So nothing. It means we didn't see much of Tony Miller and we can't tell you much about him. I'm sorry.'

'But it must have been different with Lizzie Biddick; she worked in the house and presumably came directly under you, Mrs Christophers.'

Jill concentrated on shifting her cup and saucer and the teapot into slightly different positions but said nothing. It was her husband who spoke, slowly and after due thought: 'I don't know where Lizzie comes into this, Mr Wycliffe; all I can say of the girl is that she did her work, what Jill told her to do. What else she did was her business.'

'Ralph means,' Jill said, 'there were nights when she didn't sleep in her room.'

There was a black look from husband to wife but Jill seemed not to notice.

'Isn't she the gardener's daughter?'

'Harry Biddick's daughter – yes.'

'And the Biddicks' house is just up the road, so why did the girl live in?'

It was Jill who answered. 'They're a big family, Mr Wycliffe. Lizzie is one of seven children. Her ladyship offered the girl living-in as much to help out Harry and his wife as anything else. I mean, with three bedrooms to sleep nine.'

'Is Lizzie the eldest?'

'Second. Her brother, Matt, is the eldest; he must be twenty-one or two.'

'Why did she leave?'

Christophers shrugged. 'I've no idea.'

Delicately, as though treading on tin-tacks, Wycliffe said: 'You've no idea who it was she spent those nights with?'

They both shook their heads but said nothing.

'When did she finish here?'

It was the woman who answered: 'Sunday – a week ago last Sunday. She was away early Monday morning.'

'What do you mean – "away" – isn't she back with her parents?'

Jill Christophers looked at him in astonishment. 'Back there? Not Lizzie! She was off to London. Leastwise, that's what she told everybody. All I know is she was gone from here when we got up that morning.'

Wycliffe said: 'Presumably her parents know where she is.'

The housekeeper again adjusted the position of her cup and saucer with concentrated attention. 'They know no more than anybody else. Lizzie is a very wilful girl – always been the same.'

Wyliffe tried again: 'Miller left early that same morning at the start of his holiday.'

She looked at him and the look said, as plainly as words, 'So you've got there at last!'

Early in any police investigation almost everyone concerned holds back something – secrets little or large, relevant or not. Usually the pressure of events squeezes out the truth and seemingly untellable things are eventually told, rarely with any great distress. No point then in the earnest copper getting himself into a twist and forcing the pace early on. Wycliffe drank his tea, thanked the couple, and left.

So, on the face of it, the girl had been having an affair with Miller and it certainly looked as though they had gone off together. But four days later Miller had returned. And the girl? Two days after his return Miller was murdered with an unconvincing attempt to make it look like suicide . . .

A long way to go.

It was clouding over. An end to the drought? Not according to the experts, but a weak front that might or might not produce a spitting of rain.

Chapter Six

In the police caravan Lucy Lane was going through the statements and the first of the house-to-house reports, a red felt pen poised to draw the attention of the big chief to relevant items. Daughter of a Methodist parson and a graduate in English Literature, she had made her unlikely choice of career believing that society was sick and that she must weigh in with her pennyworth on the side of healing. No sentimentalist, and a firm believer in a stick-and-carrot philosophy, the police had seemed a rational choice. Disillusionment there had been, sometimes in massive doses, but she soldiered on.

As usual the reports were thin on facts but there was enough background material to justify the exercise. The shopkeeper said: 'No good asking us about Miller, we never saw him in the village!' The publican: 'In five years he never set foot inside my bar once . . .' The vicar: 'There's a lot goes on in this village apart from the church – we've our own cricket team, there's a tennis club, a music society, a painting group . . . But the young man preferred to keep himself to himself . . .'

And there were more barbed comments: 'Ask Lord Bottrell how Miller spent his spare time,' and 'If you ask me there was something very odd about that young man . . .'

Only one person, an old maid, claimed to have heard the shot and she had no idea of the time.

Chapter and verse are rare commodities in police

work. Lucy numbered, logged, and bunched the reports for filing.

She heard the duty officer in conversation with someone in the next cubicle. They had a visitor. A head peered round her door: 'Lord Bottrell, sarge.'

His lordship came in looking self-conscious.

'I'm afraid Mr Wycliffe is not here, sir, but if I can be of any help . . .'

Bottrell stood awkwardly in the doorway of the little cubicle as though making up his mind, and then: 'May I sit down?'

There were bench seats and they faced each other across a narrow table.

'You are . . . ?'

'Detective Sergeant Lane, sir.'

'Yes, well, I've been visited by a very large young man like something out of a rugby scrum who took my fingerprints.'

'Which, Lord Bottrell, you volunteered to give.'

'Oh, I'm not complaining. It's what follows that is difficult – when you've matched my prints against others found all over the cottage – upstairs and down.'

'You were a frequent visitor?'

A flicker of irritation. 'You know damn well that I was – and why. I thought I'd better tell somebody the facts myself and not leave it all to gossip.'

His lordship was staring out of the window where the most conspicuous object was a gate pillar surmounted by one of his oh-so-discreet cats.

Lucy Lane studied her fingernails, determined not to make the next move.

'How long have you been in the force, young lady?'

'Several years.'

'So you are no stranger to the vagaries of human conduct. You may even grasp that it is possible for two men to share a deep affection each for the other which is by no means wholly sexual.' He placed a hand over his eyes as though shielding them and, after a pause, he went on in a different voice: 'In these days love is an unfashionable word but it's what I felt for Tony and, I thought, he returned.'

Then he was silent and when Lucy looked up the vaguely patronizing mask had wholly disappeared; his features were crumpled as with a child about to burst into tears.

She gave him time and when he spoke again he had to some extent regained control though he spoke slowly and with hesitation: 'It is very hard to pretend to no more than ordinary concern and a merely formal grief when most of what has seemed worthwhile in one's life is suddenly taken away . . . One is allowed to weep for a wife, even for a mistress, but not . . .' He choked over his words and broke off with a gesture of frustration. 'There is not even an acceptable word for the relationship!'

The atmosphere was becoming claustrophobic; misty rain had clouded the windows creating a sense of isolation, even of intimacy.

Lucy Lane said: 'Your words were: "I thought he returned."'

He gave her a sharp look. 'You are very perceptive and, of course, you are right. In recent weeks I've had reason to suspect that our relationship might be one-sided.'

'Reason for jealousy?'

'Yes, reason for jealousy and, by God, I was jealous!'

Lucy spoke quietly: 'So you will understand why all this is relevant to the inquiry – why what you have told me must go on record.'

He was drumming with his fingers on the table top.

'Oh, I understand . . . I understand! Why don't you caution me? "Anything you say . . ." No, that is unfair, uncalled for. I'm sorry.'

For a time they sat in silence then Bottrell said: 'There is more. I told Wycliffe that on Saturday evening I met Tony when I was out walking in South Wood.'

'That is in your statement.'

'Yes, but we had one hell of a row, and that is not in my statement.' He made an irritable movement. 'You know, I suppose, that lovers' quarrels can be among the most vicious? . . . We shouted at each other, making the wildest accusations. At one point I thought he might attack me and I hoped that he would . . .'

'Why are you telling me this?'

He looked at her. 'I don't know. Perhaps I'm trying to cover myself, on the grounds that it's better you should hear it from me than from another. You would think that on an estate like this there must be some privacy somewhere. There isn't! You are always seen by somebody; you are always overheard.'

'And were you seen or overheard on Saturday evening?'

'What? Oh, I don't know. I'm getting paranoid.'

'Of whom were you jealous?'

Bottrell hesitated. 'I'm not prepared to say; I don't want to involve another person.'

'Another man?'

'Yes.'

'It may be necessary to return to that later.'

'We shall see. I'll tell you one thing, young lady, you should have been a priest – a woman priest. You have the art of inducing confession.'

'Just one more question, sir. Does Lady Bottrell know of your association with Miller?'

A small smile. 'I think Lady Bottrell is omniscient.'

'Are you willing to make a statement embodying what you have told me?'

'Would I have come here if I wasn't?'

Wycliffe made for Miller's cottage and found Fox in the living-room, writing up his notes.

'They've been ringing around, sir, trying to get you. It's DS Shaw at sub-division.'

He put through a call and spoke to Shaw.

'Your request to CRO, sir; we've had a fax. It reads: "Subject unknown under attributed name but prints and description relate to Donald Anthony Ross convicted at Dorchester Crown Court October 1976 of assault occasioning actual bodily harm. The victim was his wife, Sharon Patricia Ross, aged 39. Ross, then 23, was sentenced to two years and released with full remission in February 1978. Request documentation if required." That's the message, sir. Puts a different complexion on things, don't you think?'

'We may need the file for the record so you'd better put in an application, but for practical purposes I can probably do better through the bush telegraph. That is Billy Norton's territory and I fancy he was already there in the seventies when this happened.'

He dropped the telephone on its cradle, given as Hercule Poirot would have said, 'furiously to think'. But Wycliffe had less confidence in his little grey cells than the Belgian.

So Miller – as Ross – had already served a sentence for assaulting his wife when he consulted Dr Bottrell after the unspecified incident in 1984. Did Bottrell know that at the time? Did he know it now? Did anyone within the Duloe orbit know? Good questions. More to the point, had Lizzie Biddick gone off with him?

And Dorchester was where Miller – he would have to

stay Miller and not Ross – had spent his short holiday. There was a pattern emerging. But had the dead man been murdered as Miller or Ross?

Fox was demanding attention. 'I'm almost through here, sir. Now I've got my report to prepare.'

'Anything fresh upstairs?'

Fox considered. 'As to prints, in the small bedroom, only the dead man's; in the other room, his, along with those of two other men.'

'None of the woman's?'

'No, sir.'

'I see. Is that all?'

'For the moment, sir.'

'Well, there's one more thing from me: I want you to check the woman's prints against those of Lizzie Biddick, a girl who, until recently, worked in the house, living in. You should find plenty of material in her room.'

Wycliffe walked back to the Incident Van. It was overcast and raining – not real rain but a fine intermittent drizzle. Probably the sun would break through again before it set. Wycliffe yearned for a real Cornish downpour; so did the jaded, parched countryside.

So Miller had a record – nothing spectacular, but it was for violence against a woman. So where did the Biddick girl fit?

In the Incident Van he found Lucy Lane, obviously anxious to tell him something, but he gave her no opportunity. He telephoned Detective Superintendent Billy Norton at Dorchester.

The usual Arab tea-party, exchanging greetings. When did we last meet? Keeping well? And Helen? . . . How is Mildred? He remembered the name in the nick of time.

'Donald Anthony Ross – mean anything to you?'

'Ross? Not off the cuff. Tell me.'

'Convicted of occasioning actual bodily harm to his wife in '76 – got two years. There's no reason why you should remember—'

'But I do! It comes back. I remember feeling a bit sorry for the boy. Not that I condone wife beating but that woman was a cow. She was God knows how much older, and if ever I saw a case of kidnapping . . . I was DI at the time; I don't recall the details but I can turn 'em up. Anyway, what's he done now?'

'Got himself murdered, apparently under an alias – Tony Miller.'

'That figures; he was a loser. Had any detail from CRO yet?'

'Not yet.'

'No, they'll probably wait for leap year or something. Anyway, I'll dig out the file, summarize the main points, and I'll fax 'em to you. By the way I heard that a DS of yours was making enquiries about a chap staying at the Crown here. Any connection?'

'That chap was our Miller – your Ross.'

'Well, I'm damned! By the way, what was he doing in your part of the world?'

'Estate foreman for Lord Bottrell.'

'That fits; I remember he was in the Parks Department here – hadn't long come down from somewhere up north.'

'Who needs files with you around?'

'We aim to please. Leave it to me.'

Wycliffe put the phone down. Lucy Lane was ostentatiously occupied. 'You gathered what that was about?'

'Not really, sir.'

Wycliffe explained and she was mollified. 'So Miller had form, and for battering a woman.'

'Yes but it doesn't make him a murderer. Anyway, there's more to it than that.' He told her about the girl,

Lizzie Biddick. 'It's an interesting thought that if that damned trigger string had been a few inches longer we might well be saying now that Miller had committed suicide in remorse and that we should be looking for the girl's body.'

'It's still possible that he killed her.'

'Oh, it's possible, and I want you to get Lady Bottrell's account of the girl; exactly what the arrangement was, what was said when she talked about leaving. Does she know of any association between the girl and Miller – or anybody else for that matter?' Wycliffe grinned. 'Woman talk, Lucy! Draw the lady out.

'Now let's have your news.'

'A couple of things, sir. There was a message from Mr Kersey to say that he's been held up but that he'll be down in the morning.'

'And?'

'Lord Bottrell has been here, baring his soul. He admits to having had a jealous quarrel with Miller when they met that Saturday evening.'

'You'd better tell me about it.'

When she had finished Wycliffe said: 'Did he give you any indication of the cause of his jealousy?'

'No, sir, he refused. I told him we might have to come back to it.'

'Perhaps this is leading us back to the Biddick girl.'

'No, he admitted that it was a man.'

'He's willing to put all this into a statement?'

'He's already done so.'

'Good! On the Miller killing, Jean Lander and the Bottrell boy are coming in to make statements. It seems the girl actually saw someone outside the cottage while young Bottrell was inside.'

By early evening the rain, such as it was, had gone, the

sky was clear and the sun shone. There is something about the Fal valley on a fine summer evening reminiscent of landscapes in biblical pictures: Adam and Eve in the garden; the lion lying down with the lamb; Ruth amid the alien corn – a timelessness, a sweet sadness. On his way back to the pub for his evening meal, Wycliffe stopped at the Biddicks' place. The land between the house and the road amounted to a small field and it was meticulously cultivated with regimented rows of broccoli, savoys, potatoes, onions, beans, carrots . . .

The voice of a male pop singer wailed in the house. A brawny, black-haired man, wearing a bib-and-brace overall and smoking a short-stemmed pipe, was hoeing between lettuces.

'Mr Biddick?'

'That's me.'

'Superintendent Wycliffe.'

Biddick spoke through his teeth, while still gripping his pipe, and went on with the hoeing. 'What can I do for you, then?'

'I want to talk to you about your daughter, Lizzie.'

Biddick paused and took the pipe from his mouth. 'Talk to the missus then, the girls is her business.' He looked at Wycliffe with dark eyes in which there was a hint of amusement. 'You'll find her in the house but I warn you, she might not be best pleased. She's cooking supper.'

The green front door, which had two little glass panes at eye level, was opened by a stockily built young man with spiky black hair and a ruddy complexion – the birdwatcher. Wycliffe had seen him down by the creek.

'You are Lizzie's brother – Matt Biddick, isn't it? . . . Superintendent Wycliffe.'

'I know who you are; I suppose you want to see Mother.' The dark eyes made it clear that soft talk was wasted. 'You best come in and I'll fetch her.'

In the living-room there was a good smell of cooking but the pop music from a vintage portable radio was raucous and deafening. Matt went through into the adjoining kitchen and before the door closed behind him Wycliffe had a glimpse of a woman's arm as she stirred something on a stove. He was not left alone, a dark girl of about sixteen was setting places on a long, narrow table. She had the bold beauty and early ripeness of a gypsy girl. If Lizzie was anything like her . . .

At one end of the table, where the cloth did not reach, a boy of nine or ten, with great concentration, was copying plant names from seed packets on to wooden labels, using a felt pen.

Wycliffe was reminded of Victorian morality prints: 'The Fruits of Industry and Thrift'. In keeping, the room was sparsely furnished but both tidy and clean. If the size of the family had led him to expect squalor and chaos he had misjudged the Biddicks.

Neither the girl nor the boy seemed to notice his presence. After an interval the door from the kitchen opened again and Mrs Biddick came in, leading a little girl by the hand and trailed by her son. 'Turn that thing off, so we can hear ourselves speak!'

It was easy to see where the good looks came from. Mrs Biddick was the sixteen year old girl, thirty years on, her figure thickened by childbearing. She said to Wycliffe: 'You can sit down.' She herself sat on a kitchen chair by the table and lifted the little girl on to her lap. Her son remained standing behind her chair.

The older girl had finished laying the table and her mother said: 'Go and keep an eye on the stew, Chris.' Then she turned to the boy with his labels. 'Leave that, Tommy. Go and help father with his weeding.'

When the two had gone, Wycliffe said: 'I'm anxious to

get in touch with your daughter, Lizzie, Mrs Biddick.'

'So am I, but I don't see what either of us can do about it.'

'You've no idea where she is?'

'London; that's where she said she was going.'

'Does she know anybody in London? Does she have some place to go?'

A slight lift of the shoulders. 'If she does, she never told me.' She reached out a hand and straightened the knife and fork at the place where she was sitting. 'It all started when she got to know Miller; she got restless – said she wanted "to better herself" and "get out of this place" – that kind of talk. She was working part-time over at the house then but her ladyship offered her full-time, living-in. It seemed a good idea; she'd have the chance to be a bit more private like – more than she could here anyway – live her own life.'

Mrs Biddick was parting her little daughter's black hair with her fingers as she spoke. 'But Lizzie was determined to break away an' that's all there is to it. She knows there's a home for her here when she wants one an' that's all I can say.'

Wycliffe was impressed by the woman's serenity, she was imperturbable as a rock, yet she seemed possessed of a broad tolerance and understanding.

The little girl on her lap was staring at Wycliffe with dark, unblinking eyes. Her mother said: 'It's rude to stare at the gentleman, Nessa!' She went on: 'Lizzie needs a man – God knows that's natural enough at her age – but there's right ways and there's wrong ways to go about it.'

Her son, standing behind her, seemed about to speak but changed his mind.

A door banged somewhere at the back of the house and yet another boy, this one about seven or eight years old, came in through the kitchen. He stood, looking from his mother to the visitor, black-eyed.

'Where's your sister?'

'She found a frog an' she's showing it to Father.'

'Go and wash your hands; supper's nearly ready.'

Wycliffe said: 'I don't want to pry into your family's affairs if they don't concern my inquiry but I must ask if you know what kind of relationship your daughter had with Mr Miller. We know that she spent time at his cottage.'

Mrs Biddick pouted. 'I wish I knew. I never really trusted that man, he was twisted, an' I don't say that because he went with men.'

'If we could find your daughter she might be able to help us with our inquiry into his death. I'm told that she left a week ago last Monday; the housekeeper and her husband say she was already gone when they got up. At the moment we know that Miller went off on his holiday early that same morning and we have to look into the possibility that she went with him.'

Matt was gripping the back of his mother's chair, tense and hostile. 'If anything's happened to Lizzie it wasn't Tony! I saw him after he came back and I asked him if he'd given her a lift. He said he hadn't seen Lizzie that morning, and I believed him.'

This spirited defence of Miller took Wycliffe by surprise, it was the very reverse of what he had expected. Even the boy's mother turned to look up at him. She said: 'Who's saying anything's happened to Lizzie, Matt? Don't get yourself worked up, boy!'

Wycliffe realized that if he was going to learn anything from the Biddicks it would be from the boy rather than the mother. He got to his feet. 'We've no reason to think that any harm has come to your daughter, Mrs Biddick, but we do need to contact her. Perhaps you could let me have a recent photograph if there is one. It would be copied and returned to you almost at once.'

Her eyes were full of suspicion. 'I don't want Lizzie's photo in all the papers and on the TV. We can do without that.'

'I promise you that we will use it with discretion.'

She lifted the little girl off her lap and crossed the room to a dresser. After searching in a drawer for a moment or two she came back with a polyfoto which she handed over.

'It's not much of a photo – one of them you take yourself: she came home with several of 'em a few months back.'

In the photograph a young woman with a mass of dark hair was smiling rather self-consciously at the camera.

Mrs Biddick saw him off at the door; her husband was nowhere to be seen; presumably he had taken refuge at the back.

Wycliffe had not gone far along the road when he heard heavy feet pounding after him and he was overtaken by Matt Biddick, breathing hard – Wycliffe suspected more from excitement than exertion.

'There's things I couldn't say in front of Mother.' He fell into step beside Wycliffe and they covered some distance before he spoke again. Then: 'You don't understand . . . I mean, Father works for Lord Bottrell like the Christophers, like Tony, and like I do sometimes . . . Then there's his tenants and they that work on the farms . . .' He paused, finding difficulty in making his point. 'I mean, people got to think of their living. It isn't like working in a factory . . . Like I say, you don't understand.'

Wycliffe said: 'I might, I was brought up in the country and my father was a tenant farmer. Our landlord was "The Colonel".'

The young man turned to him in disbelief but said nothing.

'What were you going to tell me?'

Still he hesitated. 'First they try to say Tony killed himself. Now, if anything's happened to Liz it'll be Tony who done it. He's dead, he can't defend himself, so he's fair game, and it'll let them out.'

They were interrupted by the sound of a car approaching from the village and they stood aside to let it pass: a white Mini being driven at a fair speed. Wycliffe had a glimpse of a woman at the wheel.

'Her ladyship,' the boy said. 'Now they've got something to make 'em think – her seeing me with you.'

'You were saying?'

'I was saying there's things people won't talk about; leastways not to people like you.'

'Such as?'

He plucked up courage and it came in a burst: 'Lord Bottrell was crackers about Tony – couldn't keep away. I mean, he's years older – nearly an old man, and Tony had to put up with it . . .' He broke off, confused. 'Anyway, now you know.'

The truth dawned on Wycliffe. 'But Tony preferred you; is that what you are saying?'

'And what if I am? I'm not ashamed of it. What's more, Bottrell was jealous as hell.' He added, after a pause: 'We was trying to get out.'

'To get out?'

'To start up on our own. Tony was educated, he could do all the paperwork *and* he was well up in all the horticultural stuff. Me – I can turn my hand to most anything that's practical. With a bit of capital we meant to set up in business, laying out and maintaining people's gardens. We decided to try to raise enough money to buy a van and equipment and, o'course, we would've needed somewhere to live . . .'

'You spent quite a bit of time at the cottage with Tony?'

'You could say. I used to drop in there when I was out at night – spend part of the night there.'

'So you must have known him and the cottage pretty well. I want you to go there with DS Fox and check Tony's belongings – see if you can spot anything that should be there and isn't.'

He looked doubtful. 'I don't know if I can do much, but I'll try.'

They walked a little way in silence then Wycliffe said: 'Is that all you wanted to tell me? I thought it was about your sister.'

He was getting flustered again. 'Yes, it was, but I don't know how to put it so that you take it serious. Liz was always telling me things.'

'What things?'

He clenched his fists in frustration. 'She was in with all of them . . . She knew about their goings on – things they wouldn't want talked about. I mean, Lander collects dirty pictures in that studio of his, and the doctor is having it off with—' He stopped suddenly cautious. 'Well, she had stories about all of 'em.'

'Is it possible that she made up these stories?'

He was not angry; he turned to look at Wycliffe and his expression was almost pleading. 'I knew you'd say that and it could be true, but there was something. Liz was getting money.'

'Money?'

'More than she was earning at her job anyway – a good bit more. I've seen her with a little bundle of tens and fivers more'n once. She offered me some and when I refused she said: "There's more where that came from."

O'course she was showing off but there must've bin something in it.'

'You're talking about blackmail?'

'I wouldn't be talking at all if I didn't think things needed looking into.'

'She didn't give any hint about where the money came from?'

'No, but this last few days I got to thinking . . . Well, it's possible . . . I mean, something's happened to Liz and it could be any of 'em.'

'You really think something has happened to your sister?'

'She's been gone more'n a week and she said she'd write to me as soon as she got there . . . But there's more to it than that.' He made a helpless gesture. 'I can't draw a picture! I'll tell you this: you should be trying to find her.'

They were approaching the village and they came to a halt just short of the first of the houses.

The boy said: 'I wonder sometimes if she left here at all, that's the truth of it.'

Wycliffe felt sorry for him. 'Just one question; you're a birdwatcher, a naturalist; are you out much by night?'

'Depends on the weather, three, sometimes four nights a week, I'm out for a bit. On them nights I usually finish up at Tony's – I mean I used to. There's a badger sett down in South Wood I bin watching lately; I made a bit of a hide there, but I move around . . .'

'Were you out the night Miller was killed?'

'No.'

'Do you ever meet anybody out at night?'

An amiable grin. 'I don't meet 'em because I see 'em first – not very often though. I've seen Lander a few times.'

'Doing what?'

'Nothing, just like he was out for a walk.'

'And the doctor?'

'I never see him at night – evenings he's out an' about, sometimes with a gun. He likes to pot at the pigeons.'

Wycliffe had run out of questions. 'Well, all I can promise is that we will do everything possible to find your sister.'

Wycliffe had his meal and then sat outside in the dusk, nursing a pint. Before going to bed he telephoned Helen on the guests' phone at the bottom of the bedroom stairs.

'It's me.'

'I thought it might be.'

A ritual exchange they had used on countless occasions over the years.

'Settled in all right?' Helen never asked questions requiring detailed answers over the telephone.

'I'm staying at a pub close to Duloe – just above Trelissick and the ferry – remember?'

'Of course I remember.'

They had spent a holiday in Roseland on the other side of the river. 'How's the garden?'

'Praying for rain – like me. You've only been gone about thirty-six hours so it can't have changed much.'

It was strange; when he took over an 'away' case he seemed to lose contact, to live in a different time scale. 'Of course, I'm being stupid.'

'I'm used to it. Any idea of when you'll be back?'

'Not before the weekend unless something blows up at the office.'

That night in bed he brooded for a long time before going to sleep. However he chose to put it, Lizzie Biddick had disappeared in suspicious circumstances and she had been associated with Miller, a man with a record for violence against a woman. If he had been called upon to investigate the disappearance of Lizzie Biddick with Miller still around, Miller would have been his prime suspect; the man would have been subjected to intensive questioning, every detail of his holiday would have been ferreted out and he, Wycliffe, would have had in the back of his mind the thought that it was an open and shut case.

Did the fact that Miller was dead alter this situation?

Chapter Seven

Wednesday morning, at a little after eight o'clock. As on every other morning for three weeks past the sun was shining and there was no hint of a breeze but, due to the proximity of the river and the not too distant sea, the air was moist. As the church clock chimed the quarter Wycliffe was buying his newspaper at the village shop. The landlord and the cat were at their posts. In the little square several people waited for the Truro bus: housewives with their shopping bags, young men and women – some with briefcases, on their way to work. A little way up the road sheep were being herded into a truck from a farm gate: market day in town.

As Wycliffe came out into the sunshine he felt a lift of the spirit. This was how things should be; the scale was right. He turned down the lane which led to Duloe, looking over his newspaper as he walked. At the bottom of the front page a couple of paragraphs were headed: 'Cornish Estate Murder'. The text amounted to no more than a recapitulation of the details of the crime; no mention of Lizzie Biddick, but that would come. He arrived at the Incident Van to find Kersey waiting for him.

'You must have set out at crack-of-dawn.'

'Almost; it's called being keen, sir. Anyway, somebody has sent you a naughty picture. It came by yesterday afternoon's post in an envelope addressed to "The Head of CID". I got the lab to make copies and I've brought them with me just in case. But this is the original. It's been checked for dabs and it's clean.'

The photograph was in black and white, achieving those soft half-tones which were, in part, a consequence of the long exposures necessary for indoor work before the days of fast film. The condition of the print was good though the margins were slightly foxed and there was a stain on the back. Also on the back was a number and the word, Nadar.

Kersey said: 'The lab puts the date somewhere in the eighteen-seventies. It seems this chap, Nadar, who made it, died in 1910. They think the number is a catalogue number and that it came from somebody's collection.'

The subject was a busty young girl, nude, lying on a bed or divan. At the time it was taken the photograph would have passed for art or pornography according to the eye of the beholder and the hands in which it was found. Opinion would have been slanted by the presence of pubic hair, clearly defined.

In itself the photograph was unremarkable but it had been elaborately tampered with, using colours and a very fine brush. Marks had been made in the neighbourhood of the larynx suggesting the bruising left by the thumbs after throttling, the lips had been skilfully redrawn to allow of the insertion of a protruding tongue, and the region around the eyes stippled in imitation of petechial haemorrhages. To complete the picture, areas of the face and chest had been tinted to suggest cyanosis.

Wycliffe picked up one of the copies of the photograph and slipped it into his wallet. 'Was this all there was? No message?'

'Nothing.'

'Well, whoever did this knew something about post mortem appearances after throttling, but it's hard to see why he took all that trouble simply to send it to us.

Obviously he isn't stupid enough to think we would accept it as material evidence of a crime, so what was the point? . . . Incidentally, when was it posted?'

Kersey said: 'The envelope was postmarked Monday, the day after Miller's death, but there is no collection over the weekend after Saturday midday, so it could have been posted at any time between then and first collection Monday morning.'

'Where?'

'I'll give you one guess.'

'Don't fool about.'

'The postmark says Truro. Odd, isn't it? Of course I'm not suggesting there's any connection with the Miller business.'

Wycliffe turned a mental somersault. 'No? But I'm not so sure. You don't know it, but Miller had form. Under his real name, Ross, he was convicted in '76 of occasioning actual bodily harm to his wife and sentenced to two years. Billy Norton, who handled the case, was sympathetic but it doesn't alter the fact that Miller had a conviction for violence against a woman.'

Kersey was rolling one of his cigarettes. 'So somebody with a devious mind is trying to tip us off about his record. Is that it?'

'It could be but would this photo mean anything at all to us if we didn't already know his record?'

'That's a point.' Kersey put a match to his cigarette which flared and crackled like burning straw. Wycliffe gave him a look of condescending pity.

The telephone rang and Wycliffe answered it.

'DS Fox for you, sir.'

Fox was speaking from sub-division. 'I obtained prints from the room at Duloe formerly occupied by the girl, Lizzie Biddick . . .' There was no way of stopping Fox talking as though he were in court.

'Did they match?'

'With the quantity of material in her room and in the cottage I was able to make a very thorough comparison. There is no doubt in my mind that the girl who occupied that room is the one who frequented the cottage.'

'Good! Did she leave any personal belongings in her room?'

'I didn't make a search, sir, but I saw that there were odd items of food in one of the cupboards.'

'Did Lady Bottrell or anyone else make any difficulty about you going to her room?'

'No, sir. I only saw the housekeeper; she told me where to go but she didn't come with me, nor did she ask what I wanted to do.'

As Wycliffe put the phone down Lucy Lane arrived with a tray, three mugs of coffee and a few digestive biscuits; the triumvirate was in session. Over the years they had learned to avoid each other's spines and to work together without friction or too much attention to rank. Wycliffe had never needed to trouble himself about rank; none of his people was in any doubt that he could bite as well as purr.

Outside, from time to time, villagers drifted along to stare at the cluster of police vehicles, at the van, and at Cerberus guarding the portal. But they soon got bored, and left. Fortunately the new van was fitted with one-way glass so that the inmates could see without being seen.

Wycliffe pushed the photograph to Lucy Lane with a brief explanation. She examined it for some time before passing it back. 'How very odd! Do you think there's a connection with the case?'

'That's the question; but speaking of photographs, I've got one of Lizzie Biddick; her mother gave it me and I want copies made.' He fished in his wallet and came out with the polyfoto. 'It's time we started serious enquiries; we must find out what's happened to that girl. Apart from anything else, Fox has just confirmed that prints left in her room match those found all over the place in Miller's cottage.' He passed the little photograph to Lucy Lane. 'That's her – or she, if you prefer it.'

'Will somebody tell me who we are talking about? Who is this Biddick girl?' From Kersey.

Wycliffe explained.

Lucy Lane examined the polyfoto in detail then reached for the fake. 'The two girls are very much alike. Do we have a hand lens?'

Rather shamefacedly, Wycliffe produced one from his pocket and Lucy applied herself to a fresh examination of both photographs. After a while she said: 'Both girls in these photographs are wearing pendants—'

Kersey laughed. 'Big deal! Who could ask for more?'

Unruffled, Lucy went on: 'I was going to say that the pendants are similar, though the one in the fake has been drawn in.'

'Let me see.' Wycliffe took the photographs and looked at them together. The girls were certainly alike. He went to work with his lens. In the polyfoto the pendant was plain to see: a medallion, about the size of a two-pence piece, suspended around the girl's neck by a fine chain. In the fake, a similar disc and chain had been carefully drawn in pencil. But what seemed to clinch its significance was that it carried an identical design to the one in the photograph. 'It looks,' Wycliffe said, 'like a nine and a six arranged in some sort of monogram. Of course they could be two nines or two sixes, depending on which way up you look at them . . .' He passed the photographs to Kersey. 'See for yourself.'

Kersey looked, and agreed that it was so.

Lucy Lane said: 'They're not numbers, sir. That is the

zodiacal sign for Cancer – the crab. I've seen birth-sign pendants just like this one. On the other side there would be a crab. I suppose Lizzie must have been born between June 22nd and July 22nd.'

Kersey muttered. 'Somebody is trying to tell us something but not very hard.'

Wycliffe turned to Lucy Lane: 'Did you get anywhere with Lady Bottrell over the Biddick girl?'

Lucy went on: 'I saw her last evening and received a lesson in the art of answering questions politely without saying much. At any rate I've got her version of the facts about the girl.

'It seems that Lizzie was already working in the house part-time when Lady B offered her full-time work and the chance to live in. It was intended to relieve the population pressure in the cottage where there were seven Biddicks between the ages of three and twenty-two, plus mum and dad. Added to the accommodation problem the Biddick household was being disrupted by Lizzie who was feeling her feet as a young woman and causing friction.

'The arrangement seems to have worked and there was a good prospect that the girl would settle down, but a fortnight ago, out of the blue, she announced that she was leaving and that she wanted to go almost at once. She said that she now had a chance to make a life for herself. She was grateful to the Bottrells for their help but unforthcoming about where she was going or why. Lady B talked to her mother but Mrs Biddick had had enough. "Lizzie wants to go her own way – so let her – that's what I say."'

Lucy sipped her coffee. 'Then, a week ago last Saturday, Lizzie told Lady Bottrell she would be leaving on the Monday, catching the 10.30 London train from Truro. On Sunday, Lady Bottrell gave her her wages, her fare, and a cash leaving present. She also offered to drive her to the station next morning and Lizzie accepted but, in the morning when it was time for them to be leaving, Lady B went in search of her and found that she'd already gone.'

Wycliffe asked: 'But nobody actually saw her leave?'

'No, sir. They simply assumed she must have gone because she wasn't around.'

'And Miller left that same morning. According to Lord Bottrell he must have been away, in his car, before eight o'clock. The obvious conclusion, though not necessarily the right one, is that they went off together.'

Wycliffe recounted his interviews with the Christophers and with Lizzie's family. 'The housekeeper says there were nights when Lizzie didn't sleep in her room and she obviously thought the girl spent those nights with Miller. But the point is, if she went off with Miller, she didn't come back with him.'

Kersey had been unusually silent, trying to come to terms with a case of which he was hearing the detail for the first time. Now he drained his coffee mug and reached for another biscuit. He tapped the photograph with the edge of his biscuit. 'With Miller's record this could be what happened to the poor little fool and some oddball is trying to tell us about it in his own way. It seems to me we need to know more about Lizzie's last days in Duloe and whether they were her last days anywhere.'

Wycliffe agreed. 'We need to know whether she caught a London train or any other. If Miller was involved, did he merely drop her off at Truro station? Did he leave his car in the park there and travel on by rail either with her, or alone? As things stand we've no conclusive evidence that the girl left here at all.'

'But if she's still here . . .'

'Don't let's get carried away . . .' Wycliffe broke off and his expression changed. 'Having in mind what her brother told me, it seems to me unlikely that she was having an affair with Miller and it's just occurred to me that Fox found no trace of her in the upstairs rooms. It's difficult to understand why, if they were having an affair, they confined their activities to the living-room and the kitchen when there were two good beds upstairs.'

Lucy Lane said: 'It doesn't make sense.'

'No, it doesn't. We are not there yet. For the moment let's remember that we have a dead man who was shot but we don't have a dead girl who was throttled; all we have is a much doctored photograph of a young woman who lived a century ago.'

He turned to Lucy Lane. 'For a start, I want you, Lucy, to take a good look at her room at Duloe. Find out if she left anything behind and see what you can get from Jill Christophers; she'll be more likely to talk when her husband is not there . . . And you, Doug – I want you to get somebody to pick up the girl's trail between here and Truro, that Monday morning. If she made the trip she must have been seen. I know ten days is a long time but we've got to try. Also see if the railway people can tell us anything. Another thing: arrange for Miller's car – it's in the old coach house – to be gone over by Fox. You'd better have it transferred to a garage at sub-division.'

Most cases have a distinguishing feature or perhaps an atmosphere which long afterwards comes vividly to mind whenever the case is mentioned. He was beginning to think that in this instance it would be a sense of stillness and of isolation. He was always aware of the river and the creeks on three sides. Although the village was close at hand it was all too easy to imagine that the estate and the lawyer's house were cut off; self-contained, autonomous.

It affected his thinking, inclining him to restrict his search for explanations to the Bottrells, the Landers, and their appendages, as though they existed in a closed community.

Now he was in search of another Lander – Lander père – the old man he had met briefly during his visit on that first evening. His spies in the Incident Van had reported Simon leaving for the office as usual and, half an hour later, his wife, Beth, had driven off in her little Fiat. So there was a chance of catching the old man alone.

He walked down the gravelled drive and rang the door bell but his only achievement was to set the dog barking. Then he heard the whine of an electric motor not far away and he set off around the house. The sound came from a large brick-built shed in the kitchen yard. The door was open so he coughed loudly to announce himself and went in.

Lander senior was seated on a stool at a bench fitted with a variety of power tools for small-scale work in wood. At the moment he was turning a slender shaft on a tiny lathe. On the windowsill at the back of the bench, plastic boxes in rows were labelled: Detached shafts, Column bases, Capitals, Arch mouldings . . .

He stood for a full minute with no acknowledgement of his presence and was beginning to think that he was invisible when Lander removed the shaft from the lathe chuck and dropped it into the appropriate box. His bony fingers, despite enlarged joints, were nimble and precise. He turned on his stool to face Wycliffe. 'Now, sir!'

His grey overall was powdered with wood dust which had also become trapped in his moustache and even speckled his cheeks and the lenses of his spectacles. But the grey eyes were alive.

'Interested?'

'Intrigued.'

'Then take a look through that door.'

The door led into another section of the shed, the floor of which was largely taken up with the model of a church or, more likely, a cathedral, under construction. The outer walls reached only to window level but the nave arcade was complete on the north side and in process of erection along the south aisle.

'I'm building a cathedral on a scale of one thirty-second. When I was a boy I wanted to be an architect but family tradition made me a lawyer. In any case they wouldn't have let me loose on cathedrals. Now I can please myself . . . You see, I shall virtually complete the interior before I get far with the exterior walls . . . I shall make the roof removable in sections so that one can see all the goodies inside . . . Of course there will be a tower at the crossing . . . I machine those parts which lend themselves to it but the mouldings, capitals, bosses, corbels, etcetera involve carving which is a trial for old fingers and old eyes . . .'

The old man's voice was thin and rather high-pitched; words came tumbling out as damned up enthusiasm found its vent. Wycliffe recognized the danger and began to draw away from further involvement. It took time but he managed it and they returned to the workshop where Wycliffe was given a stool.

'I'm surprised that you found me here; I suppose you wanted Simon?'

'No, I assumed that he would be at his office.'

Wycliffe was sizing him up: an elderly, retired professional man, absorbed in his hobby, inclined to be garrulous, and reaching an age when even the most dramatic and tragic events were losing their emotional impact, their cutting edge – the 'I've seen it all before' syndrome.

But he saved Wycliffe from having to bring the subject

around to the crime. He removed his spectacles and began to clean them with a grubby handkerchief and while he was watching Wycliffe with unfocused eyes he said: 'Do you really believe, Mr Wycliffe, that Miller was murdered?'

'There is very little room for doubt, I'm afraid.'

Lander put his spectacles back on and turned his gaze on Wycliffe. 'It seems from the little I know that there are only two pieces of evidence pointing to murder: first, that the string to the trigger was too short for him to reach; second, that he was left-handed whilst the set-up suggested a right-handed person.' He broke off. 'Of course you will have access to facts not available to me . . .' The grey eyes were innocent and enquiring.

Wycliffe was cautious. 'You don't find the facts you have mentioned convincing?'

He did not answer directly. 'Well, it's true that Tony had a tendency to left-handedness but, in fact, he was ambidextrous. He sometimes helped me with delicate little jobs in assembly which are getting too much for my old fingers and his either-handedness was invaluable. I don't think he would have troubled too much about which hand he used to pull the trigger.'

'You saw a good deal of him?'

'He looked in fairly often. He was interested in what I am doing.'

'But what about the short string? Do you have any explanation of that?'

The old man seemed to smile under the luxuriance of his moustache. 'You don't think, Mr Wycliffe, that in this case you may have an unusual factor at work – a mischievous person with no other motive than to complicate matters and make trouble?' Lander senior was garrulous but he was not a fool.

'Are you suggesting that someone found the dead man

and deliberately cut the string to mislead any investigation?'

'You are quick to grasp the implication, sir. You think, perhaps, that it is a possibility to be considered?'

'If I said yes, would this "imp of the perverse" have a name?'

Lander laughed outright. 'My dear sir, I can name you no names! I merely offer an idea, a suggestion – an alternative to the rather frightening possibility that we have a murderer in our midst.'

Wycliffe was uncomfortable; the sun streamed through the windows of the workshop and he was sweating though Lander remained, to all appearances, serenely cool. At the same time Wycliffe felt mentally adrift; he sensed that there was something to be gained by talking to this man but only if he could interpret what was said and discern some motive behind it. All he could do was to play the game and guess at the rules.

'Perhaps there is another point which favours murder: Dr Bottrell knew Miller both as a man and a patient and he is strongly of the opinion that Miller was an unlikely suicide.'

Lander nodded. 'That doesn't surprise me – I mean the fact that James said so doesn't surprise me.'

'I see.'

Another nod, this time emphatic. 'Yes, I really think you do.' He sat, waiting, looking Wycliffe straight in the eyes. It was almost a challenge, as if he would say: 'If you want me to tell you something you must find the right questions.'

Wycliffe tried a fresh approach. 'I, of course, am a stranger. Until a few days ago I knew nothing of the people I am now meeting. It would be a great help if you would tell me something of the two families – the Bottrells and your own.'

'With pleasure.' He seemed to mean it. 'We have acted for the family since we set up a law practice in Truro in the 1830s.' A brief smile. 'Before Victoria came to the throne. It was nearly seventy years later, at the turn of the century, that my grandfather bought a piece of land from the estate and built this house. Since then we have been neighbours.'

An observation seemed to be required. 'Your son and the present Lord Bottrell seem to get on remarkably well.' It sounded weak but it curtailed the history lesson and produced a broad smile.

'That's easily explained; they are the same age, they went to the same schools, they did their National Service and then went up to Oxford together. In other words they are, and always have been, good friends.'

'And I suppose that Lord Bottrell's twin brother, James, made up the trio?'

A tremor of uncertainty; a sensitive spot? But the old man's response when it came was smooth enough: 'Poor James was unlucky. While still very young he developed a tubercular lesion in the joint of his left knee – you must have noticed that he is markedly lame. However, on the credit side, he had the good fortune to be among the first to benefit from the then wonder drug – streptomycin. It worked, and further progress of the disease was halted.'

The old man brushed sawdust from the sleeve of his overall. 'But he had suffered a serious setback to his education and development. His illness forced him to drop out of his age group – no boarding school, no games, no National Service, and only a very belated entry to university. But, as you know, he caught up and certainly outdistanced the others academically.'

Wycliffe, anxious to pick some plums out of this pie, risked a question or two. 'When did he give up his consultancy and come here to live?'

'When his Aunt Cecile died and her money made it possible. That was two years ago.'

'Wasn't it a little odd? Coming back here to live in his brother's backyard so to speak?'

The old man grinned. 'Not if you remember that, as an unmarried man, he had no other real home. Although Hugh inherited the estate it was still the place where James was born and brought up.'

Something in the old man's manner seemed to indicate a readiness for other questions.

'When did the present Lord Bottrell inherit?'

'Nine – no, ten years ago.'

'Was his mother still alive?'

'Very much so! She died only a couple of years back – within weeks, actually, of her sister-in-law, Aunt Cecile.' A ruminative chuckle. 'I doubt if James would have come back had his mother been still around.'

'They didn't get on?'

The old man waved a thin hand. 'Families, Mr Wycliffe! Her ladyship was possessed of a very dominant personality and I'm afraid that she discriminated most blatantly between her two sons. Hugh could do no wrong – he was something of a mother's boy – while poor James . . . Ah, well!'

The sigh was unconvincing and Wycliffe was sure that he had been deliberately fed with certain facts under the guise of indiscretions from a garrulous old man.

Wycliffe tried one more throw: 'There is just one other question, Mr Lander, then I will leave you to get on with your work. I shall be interested in anything you can tell me about the girl, Lizzie Biddick.'

The old man looked at him in surprise, genuine or simulated. 'Biddick? You are talking about the gardener's eldest girl. She worked in the house – I believe she lived in for a few months – one of Cynthia's protégées, I think. Anyway she left quite recently – went to London, so they tell me. Why? Is she concerned in this Miller affair?'

Wycliffe left it at that.

He walked back to the Incident Van brooding. Although there was little that was specific he felt that he had come away with something more than the conviction that Lander père was a wily customer. He mulled over what he had been told, trying to extract the meat. Some source of friction between James, on the one hand, and his brother and Lander on the other? In the end he settled for a muttered: 'They're an odd lot!' And a few paces farther on he added: 'Very odd!'

Jill Christophers said: 'This part was altered by Lord Bottrell's grandfather when they were still two or three housemaids living in. The only way into the family's rooms from here is through that door and Ralph has to make sure that's locked at night.'

She and Lucy Lane were standing in a little hall beside the kitchen.

'Upstairs on the next landing is our flat, then there's another flight, and on that floor there's a bathroom and three more rooms; Lizzie had one of them.'

'And the other two?'

Jill shrugged. 'Store rooms, junk really.'

The housekeeper asked no questions; in fact, throughout the inquiry so far, Lucy had been asked very few questions. People answered more or less readily what they were asked, then waited as though anxious for a minimum of involvement. A pity, for as Wycliffe frequently reminded her, questions are sometimes more informative than answers.

'Lizzie had a key?'

'To the little door beside the kitchen. That reminds

me, if you're going up you'd better have her room key. I locked it until we know what's to be done with the things she left behind.'

Lucy went upstairs. On the first landing there was a single door to the Christophers' flat, then the stairs continued to the next landing where there were four doors, one of them locked, and that was the girl's room. One thing was clear; Lizzie could have come and gone as she wished, day or night, disturbing no-one.

The room was furnished with heavy pieces, evidently brought from other and larger rooms elsewhere in the house: a mahogany wardrobe, an ornate walnut dressing-table, a chest of drawers, and a bed with brass rails. But there was a basin with hot and cold water, an electric fire, and a gadget for making coffee. Lucy recalled the cheerless, draughty attic which had been hers at university (no washing facilities; lavatory and bathroom two flights down) and thought Lizzie had done pretty well for herself.

Lucy made a start on the wall cupboard next to the washbasin: some oddments of china and cutlery, a can-opener, a box of shredded wheat, a jar of instant coffee, a packet of sugar, a bottle of milk half-full and curdled . . .

She turned to the wardrobe which was empty except for a little pile of books tied about with string. Lucy slid them out and looked at the titles: a mixed bag – Thomas Hardy's *Jude the Obscure*, Lawrence's *Sons and Lovers*, John Updike's *The Witches of Eastwick*, and Yukio Mishima's *Forbidden Colours*. Each of them had Miller's name on the flyleaf. Lucy wondered what Lizzie Biddick had made of that lot; a remedy for innocence in four not-so-easy lessons.

The dressing-table was clear but the glass top was smeared with lipstick and face cream. A wastepaper basket contained used tissues, a drinks can and some sweet papers. On the face of it the room had been vacated by a girl who cared nothing for the impression she left behind. But there was another interpretation: that when Lizzie last left her room she did so with every expectation that she would be back to complete her packing, perhaps to tidy up, perhaps to return the borrowed books.

In which case . . .

Lucy sat on the bed, looking about her, wondering if she had missed anything. People put things on the tops of wardrobes. She stood on a chair, reached in over the fretted rail and came out with a large shoulder bag, almost new. It was limp and apparently empty. She zipped it open on the bed – nothing, but in one of the side pockets she found a wallet-purse and a building society passbook.

The building society account had been opened about a year earlier and followed by small deposits of a few pounds at a time, but more recently larger sums had been credited so that the balance now stood at well over a thousand pounds.

Lucy muttered to herself: 'Not on her wages!'

The purse held a hundred and twenty pounds in fives, tens and twenties, a single, standard-class ticket to London, and a seat reservation for the 10.30 train on the day she was supposed to have left.

It was enough.

Lucy was not so hardened that she felt no sympathy with or distress for this silly girl. She went downstairs and found Jill Christophers in the kitchen working fruit into a cake mixture in a large, stainless steel bowl. 'His lordship is very fond of fruit cake but he can't abide the shop stuff.'

'Lizzie left some of her belongings in her room.'

'Really? Your policeman said there were books in the wardrobe; I haven't looked. I just locked the door until her ladyship tells me what she wants done. I've been here long enough to know better than take anything on myself.'

'When did you last see her, Mrs Christophers?'

Jill paused in her mixing. 'I've got to think . . . It was Sunday evening; I went up to her room to ask her to square up for some batteries Ralph bought for her radio.'

'Did she seem her usual self?'

Pursed lips. 'As far as I could see. She was packing. There was a big hold-all on the floor, bulging with stuff and another she was working on. I said to her: "You won't get much more in that."'

'What sort of hold-alls were they?'

'Those blue canvas things with leather straps.'

'And that was the last time you saw her?'

She hesitated. 'No, it wasn't. It's just come back to me. I saw her later in the evening – about half-nine it must've bin. Ralph was watching the telly and I had one or two things to do down here. As I was coming out of our flat I met her on the landing.'

'Did you speak to her?'

'Just what you'd expect. She said she was going out for a bit of fresh air.'

'Can you recall how she was dressed?'

A shrug. 'Casual. Not for going anywhere special: dark-blue slacks and an orange blouse. It was a warm evening but she wasn't going far like that.'

'Was she carrying anything?'

'I think she had her handbag but I couldn't swear to it.'

'You didn't see her again, but did you hear her?'

'Yes, I did: her room is right over our bedroom and I heard her moving about up there. I thought she was finishing her packing.'

'Any idea of the time?'

She frowned. 'I do, as a matter of fact. I'd had my first sleep and I looked at the clock; it was five minutes past one . . . Be a dear an' roll up my sleeve, it's slipping into the mix.'

Lucy did as she was asked. 'Just one more question, Mrs Christophers, does Lizzie wear a pendant with her birth sign?'

'Always; it's one of her things; she's daft about the stars and all that; her horoscope is the first thing she looks at in the paper.'

'Do you know her birthday?'

A quick smile. 'July 4th – Independence Day – she seemed to think that made her something special – silly girl!'

When there were no guests the Bottrells had their meals in the breakfast-room which was conveniently close to the kitchen. It was a shabby little room but it overlooked the park with glimpses of the river and it caught the morning sun. As usual, at midday the table was set for four and the food was laid out under covers. There was a heated trolley for hot dishes and the family arrived as it suited them.

At 12.30 Lord and Lady Bottrell had the room to themselves. Lord Bottrell helped himself to soup from the trolley while Lady Bottrell, already at table, sprinkled hers with Parmesan cheese.

Lady Bottrell said: 'Have you seen the papers this morning?'

'I glanced through the *Telegraph* – nothing about Tony.'

'You should have tried the tabloids. "Our correspondent understands that Lord Bottrell is deeply distressed by the crime. It seems that the two men were close friends so that their relationship was more intimate than is usual between employer and employed . . ." That's a quote and just a sample.'

'You know where that came from: your father has been talking.'

Lady Bottrell broke off a morsel of bread and put it into her mouth. 'They don't need him. Anybody in the village would do as well. I warned you, Hugh.'

'You warned . . . !' He had started angrily but broke off. 'I'm sorry, Cynthia, but this is a nightmare.' He brought his soup to the table and sat staring at it as though mesmerized.

'You know that Jean lied to the police and that Paul is involved?'

'Yes. I suppose Paul told you; I had to hear it from Lander.'

Lady Bottrell spooned up a little soup and raised it to her lips where it vanished soundlessly. She patted her lips with a napkin, then: 'Hugh, was Lander giving Lizzie money?'

Bottrell had picked up his spoon, now he put it down again. 'For God's sake, Cynthia, how would I know?'

The door opened and James Bottrell came in. 'What is it today?' He lifted one of the covers. 'Ham like soggy blotting paper. Why can't we have ham off the bone, Cynthia?'

Lady Bottrell was chilling. 'We can if you like to pay for it and, perhaps, cook it, James.'

James helped himself to soup and sat down. 'So now young Paul has got himself tangled in the Lander net.'

Chapter Eight

Kersey said: 'Lizzie Biddick found out that Miller was an ex-con and blackmailed him. She went to see him that Sunday night to collect, perhaps, a final instalment before she went away, but instead of paying he throttled her and disposed of the body. The following day he set off on his holiday but came back early, scared and conscience stricken. On the Sunday night, exactly a week after murdering the girl, he shot himself. How's that?'

Wycliffe looked at him. 'Did you think that up all by yourself? For one thing, how did he manage to shoot himself?'

Kersey made a broad gesture. 'You can make too much of that bit of string. Maybe it was too short for him to reach with his hand but he might have caught it round his foot. I reckon I could do it.'

'Perhaps you should try rolling your cigarettes that way.'

Lucy Lane had long since learned to recognize Kersey's excursions into fantasy as Aunt Sallys, designed to set going an argument. They were having lunch at the pub, at the table in the alcove which Wycliffe had made his own. They were served with the dish-of-the-day, a prawn salad with fresh prawns which Kersey could not peel. 'Damn it! Joan always does it for me.'

Lucy reached for his plate. 'Give them to me!'

Wycliffe said: 'How much of that nonsense you talked just now do you believe?'

Kersey grinned. 'Well, perhaps not all, but I reckon there's a core of truth.'

Lucy sipped her apple juice. 'Anyway, the pendant Lizzie wore makes it pretty certain that whoever sent the doctored photograph intended to suggest a connection.'

Kersey agreed. 'It also means that he knew more than was good for him. So are we looking for the girl or her body?'

Wycliffe hesitated. 'We musn't forget that Miller could have sent the photograph himself; we know that it could have been posted at any time after midday on Saturday. As to whether we are looking for the girl or her body: for public consumption we are investigating a suspicious disappearance but we shan't be able to keep that up. The time has come to get a team together and search for her body. I want you to organize it, Doug. Of course you'll need men from sub-division and a dog handler. Arrange it through Reed.'

Kersey said: 'We've had one positive response so far on the Biddick trail – a clerk in the travel centre at Truro Station remembers her buying her ticket and reserving a seat on the Friday before she was due to travel on the Monday. He was struck by the fact that it all seemed new to her; she seemed quite flustered about making a trip for which most people wouldn't bother to make a forward booking.'

Wycliffe left the pub and walked back to the Incident Van, glad of the fresh air to minimize the soporific effect of a couple of glasses of Chablis. Dixon, the duty officer, handed him an official envelope. 'The pathologist's report, sir, by messenger. And Dorchester CID phoned: Superintendent Norton will be out for most of the rest of the day and could you ring him before he leaves.'

'Get him for me, please.'

The pathologist's report was mainly important as

documentation. Unless a pathologist is bloody minded (and Franks was not), anything worth knowing has been passed on by phone before the report is in type. He skimmed the technical jargon and put the report aside for filing. After all, from a pathological angle there is little new that can be said of an otherwise healthy man who has been blasted by a shotgun discharged at short range.

Norton came on: 'I've put through the promised fax to your sub-division – just a précis of the main points from the file. I've also had a report from our chap who's been looking into the Ross/Miller visit. They remember him at the Crown. He arrived, alone, on the Monday morning and left his car in the hotel car park. Apart from breakfast he had only one meal in the hotel during his stay: that was on Tuesday evening when he dined there with a woman of about his own age. The staff remember her as sophisticated and well turned out, not quite his style.'

Norton paused for breath. 'The file reminded me that he had a sister in Dorchester at the time of his trial – Olivia Ross, and this could have been her. We haven't traced her yet but we'll keep trying. By the way, was he still playing the flute?'

'Yes, why?'

'Only that counsel for defence – still wet behind the ears – made a lot of that. Finally the judge – old Itchy – you remember Itchy? – looked over his half-glasses and said: "Am I to understand that counsel is advancing this accomplishment of the defendant as testimony to his rectitude and good conduct?"'

Wycliffe felt broody, in need of time to ponder but, as in Elizabethan drama, it was time for the clowns; the TV team had arrived and he was required to stand outside the van, squinting in the sunshine.

He said that the inquiry was continuing, that there was

no immediate prospect of an arrest but that a number of leads were now being followed. He added, tongue-in-cheek, that he had been impressed by the co-operation of the public.

Then the interviewer sprang his question. 'Is it true that you are trying to contact Miss Lizzie Biddick who formerly worked at Duloe?'

'Yes, we would like to talk to Miss Biddick.'

'Would you say that she has disappeared?'

'In the sense that we don't know where she is. She left her employment after giving proper notice but she did not leave a forwarding address.'

'You have no reason to think that anything has happened to her?'

'I have no evidence that she is not alive and well if that is what you mean.'

'Do you think that there may be a connection between her leaving and the murder of Tony Miller?'

'Our reason for wanting to talk to her is that she knew Mr Miller very well and might, therefore, be a helpful witness.'

And with that the media dragon was temporarily appeased.

Wycliffe was disturbed. Tony Miller had been found dead in circumstances which suggested suicide. A closer look had caused the investigating officer to revise that first impression. For suicide it was necessary to read probable homicide. At that stage he, Wycliffe, had taken over; a straightforward killing complicated only by the rigged suicide. So two questions had needed answers: Why was Miller killed? And by whom?

Then a dotty picture, among other things, had brought Lizzie Biddick into the case. Lizzie, it seemed, was a footloose girl, sexually attractive, searching for something without knowing what, and possibly engaged in a spot of blackmail. But she had disappeared from the scene days before Miller's death. Now, instead of that death, Wycliffe found himself concentrating on the girl's disappearance. He was confused; there was a risk of proceeding to run around in ever decreasing circles, perhaps with the classic consequence. He must clear his mind and lay down definite lines on which to proceed.

On the principle that onlookers see most of the game he decided on another talk with James Bottrell. But was James a mere onlooker? Whether he was or not he was a shrewd observer and even his biased and distorted observations could be instructive.

Once more he rapped on the varnished plank door of the little house in the old stable yard but this time there was no reply and the door was shut. After a second and a third attempt he heard footsteps inside, the door opened and Bottrell was standing there looking vaguely dishevelled and off balance. 'Ah! It's you . . . You'd better come in.'

Wycliffe followed him into the hall-like room; it was much as he had seen it before except that the cover was on the typewriter and there was no sign of work in progress.

'I usually take a nap after lunch; I suppose it's a sign of approaching old age.'

'I'm sorry to have disturbed you.'

They sat as before, facing each other across the table. A slight sound caused Wycliffe to look up at the gallery. A woman was standing in the doorway of one of the rooms, almost in silhouette, but the light shone on her blonde hair and caught the silky folds of the bedroomy thing she wore. It lasted only for an instant, then the door closed, but Wycliffe was in no doubt that the woman was Cynthia Bottrell.

Bottrell glanced up but he was too late. 'Well, what

can I do for you?' He had recovered his poise.

Without comment Wycliffe handed over the photograph of the nude girl with its imaginative additions.

Bottrell studied the photograph in detail. 'Where did you get this?'

'It's a copy of one sent to me anonymously, through the post.'

'It's kinky.'

'Is that a professional opinion?'

Bottrell chuckled. 'You realize the original was probably taken in the last century?'

'I've been told so, but it is the additions which interest me; the pendant which has been sketched in is similar to one worn by Lizzie Biddick – it has her birth sign on it.'

Bottrell re-examined the photograph with care. 'Odd! This girl is vaguely like Lizzie. Anyway, whoever made the amendments knew what he was about, medically speaking if not artistically.' He looked up. 'Have you shown this to Lander?'

'Should I have done?'

'As I told you, Lander is a photographic buff and he's interested in the history of photography. At least he collects old photographs – originals when he can afford them, copies when he can't. I'm sure he would be interested in the original of this.'

Wycliffe could see that the door which had closed behind Lady Bottrell was once more open – just a crack. She was listening, and Bottrell must have known that she would be.

Bottrell looked quizzical: 'You have some reason, other than this photograph, to be interested in the Biddick girl?'

'We found a considerable sum of money and other things in her room which she would not willingly have left behind; also, and significantly, her rail ticket.'

'So you are wondering if this photograph was intended as a message.'

'Yes.'

Bottrell lit a cigarette and dribbled smoke into the air. 'You think something has happened to the girl?'

'It seems likely.'

'When did you get this?'

'It was posted in this district during last weekend.'

Bottrell seemed thoughtful. 'You suspect Miller?'

'Should I?'

A movement of slight impatience. 'I've no data on which to form an opinion.'

Wycliffe said, as though the remark was a casual one: 'I thought you might have more data than most.'

Bottrell's expression hardened. 'Will you explain that?'

'Instead I will ask you another question: Did you know Tony Ross?'

There was a longish pause, then Bottrell spoke, picking his words with care: 'I know that Miller changed his name from Ross.'

'How do you know?'

'He told me.'

'When?'

'When he first came to consult me.'

'Did he tell you why?'

Bottrell fiddled with papers on thc tablc in front of him. 'He didn't need to. It's a phenomenon every psychologist comes across in his work, a desire on the part of someone who has endured a traumatic crisis to change his or her name, to escape, symbolically, from an identity which has been imposed and has become distasteful.'

'Or inconvenient.'

A faint smile. 'You choose to be cynical but this

distaste is real enough. The image of ourselves that we present to the world is not of our own choosing or wholly of our own making and it usually differs dramatically from our self-image—'

Wycliffe cut in without ceremony: 'Miller, as Ross, had a criminal record. Did he tell you that he had served a gaol sentence for assaulting his wife?'

Bottrell paused in the act of raising his cigarette to his lips. 'He did not.'

Wycliffe wondered what Cynthia Bottrell was making of this conversation. He stole a glance up at the gallery. A line of light showed that the door was still open. Bottrell seemed oblivious or indifferent.

Wycliffe decided to change the subject. 'Lizzie Biddick was getting money from somebody.'

'Blackmail?'

'If Miller killed himself we would have a credible interpretation of the sequence of events: Lizzie is extracting money from Miller under threat of disclosing his true identity; he kills her and later, out of fear or remorse or both, he kills himself.'

'But Miller didn't kill himself.'

'The only material evidence against it is that the trigger string was too short.'

'So?'

'It has been suggested that someone discovered the body and cut the string before, or even after, young Paul entered the cottage that night.'

'Surely that is absurd! What possible motive could there have been?'

'I admit that with a motive the idea might be more credible, but the facts are that the shot which killed Miller was fired at approximately 12.30. It was after 1.30 that Paul went into the cottage and saw the body. While he was in there, Jean Lander, waiting outside, saw a man lurking close to the cottage. If that man was the killer, what was he doing there an hour after the shot? If he was not the killer, what was he doing there anyway? I would give a good deal to know who that man was.'

They looked at each other across the table. Bottrell said: 'I'm afraid I can't help you there.'

'And yet the list of possible candidates must be a very short one.'

Bottrell stubbed out his cigarette. 'You think so? All sorts of people wander around this place at night. God knows why.'

Wycliffe changed the subject. 'I talked to Lander senior this morning.'

'And he showed you his cathedral?'

'He did. He also told me about your unfortunate illness as a child.'

Bottrell's face lost all expression. 'Did he! Well, that was a long time ago.'

Something there. Wycliffe sat back in his chair, missing his pipe. These moments came at longer and longer intervals but when they did the sense of deprivation was still acute.

Bottrell was watching him. 'May I ask if this is the end of a round or the end of the contest?'

Wycliffe ignored the question. 'Did Lizzie Biddick come here?'

Bottrell lit another cigarette. 'Ah! Merely an interval! I was wondering if we might get to that. Yes, she did.'

'Often?'

'Several times, anyway. Lizzie was – is, for all I know – desperately anxious to be noticed. It's not uncommon, especially amongst women; many of them construct some private mythology through which they come to terms with their insignificance; others need an external prop. When Lizzie discovered that, as well as being a psychologist, I had a medical degree, I became an irresistible target.'

'What did it amount to?'

Bottrell grinned. 'A need to talk, a need to impress. The confessional is a great institution for straightening out psychological kinks. A good priest is worth his weight in gold because he gives his people time, and he listens. His penitents come away convinced that their sins, at least, are important.'

'Getting back to the girl . . .'

'Yes, well, she turned up here one evening, latish, saying she was worried about a pain in her left breast and that she hated going to her GP. I didn't intend to fall for that one – not so early in our acquaintance anyway – so I fetched the gin bottle and we talked. Or she talked. As I say, she came back several times, presumably for more of both.'

'Did you ever get around to her pain?' Wycliffe allowed his curiosity to get the better of him.

A thin smile. 'She forgot about it.'

Up in the gallery the line of light was still visible, marking the open door.

'When did you last see her?'

'The Sunday evening before she left – or intended to leave. She came to say goodbye.'

'At what time was this?'

'It must have been coming up for ten.'

Wycliffe was looking at him with an expressionless stare, neither penetrating nor aggressive, but bland.

Bottrell said: 'All right, I've just realized it myself! I was the last person to admit having seen Miller alive, and now . . .' He smiled a whimsical smile. 'I suppose it must mean something. It's up to you to decide what.'

'Who was she getting money from?'

'I've no idea. Certainly not from me.' He raised his arms, braced his shoulders, and suppressed a yawn. 'I've said that Lizzie talked, but she didn't tell me anything. Most of it was pure fantasy – how her school teachers begged her mother to let her stay on at school. "They said I'd be sure to get to Oxford." Another time it was how, at fifteen, she'd been raped by a famous TV star, down here on holiday, and her parents had been paid to hush it up. Another version was that the TV chap had offered her a part in one of his shows to hold her tongue but she'd turned it down . . . The stories were different each time but variations on a theme: people notice me, therefore I'm real. An amendment to Descartes.'

'Did she tell you that she was going to London?'

'Oh, yes. I pointed out that it was a big place and asked her if she knew anybody there. She said that she did and that "he" would be her protector, so there was no need to worry.'

'She told you nothing about her life at Duloe, and about her relations with Miller?'

'Nothing, and I didn't ask. The girl needed to unwind and that is what she did. That, with a glass or two of gin to make her slightly tipsy, was her therapy.'

Wycliffe stood up. 'I am beginning to envy your patients, Dr Bottrell, and I'm sure that I shall need to hear more of this one.'

'You know where to find me.'

He saw Wycliffe to the door then returned to his seat at the table.

A moment later Cynthia Bottrell looked over the gallery rail. She came down slowly – Woman Descending a Staircase – but it was lost on Bottrell who did not look up. Her dressing gown was of blue silk, she had not a hair out of place, and she moved with languid elegance like a romantic actress approaching her big scene.

'Do you think he saw me?'

'I've no idea.'

'If he did, will he tell Hugh?'

'Why should he?'

She said without aggression: 'You don't care a damn, do you?' She ran her fingers through his hair. The dressing gown had slipped open exposing her breasts. 'All you want from me is a good lay.'

'And you need to be laid. So what? You don't want a husband, you've already got one, and it would be a pity to give up being a ladyship – you do it so well.' He looked up at her. 'In any case we are both a bit long in the tooth for romance.'

His manner was playful rather than overtly cruel but a deep flush spread upwards over her fair skin. She pulled her dressing gown about her and looped the sash. 'You are a real bastard, James!'

She fiddled with an untidy heap of papers on the table, boxing them together. 'Does Wycliffe really believe that Tony Miller committed suicide?'

'Of course he doesn't!'

'That photograph he showed you . . . Where did it come from?'

'Why ask me? In any case it's not difficult to guess.'

She was silent for a while, then asked: 'What about Lander, James?'

Bottrell reached for his cigarettes. 'What about him? At the moment Simon is not a happy man and I doubt if his prospects will improve.'

Another pause, and then she said: 'I'm scared, James. There are so many questions I'm afraid to ask.'

'Then don't ask them.'

'Tell me one thing: is the Biddick girl dead?'

'How should I know? Wycliffe evidently thinks so.'

She ran a finger up the nape of his neck, lifting his hair. 'Did you screw her?'

'I can't remember.'

'Pig!' She looked at her watch. 'It's only a quarter past three and Hugh won't be home before six; we could go upstairs again.'

He looked at her with a small satisfied smile. 'Is that all you think about?'

'I'm afraid to think of much else.'

Lucy Lane was in the van. 'I've had young Bottrell and the Lander girl here to make their statements, sir. They're like babes in a wood.'

Wycliffe was in no mood for sentiment. 'I'm glad there are some innocents in this case even if they are also liars. That Bottrell brother is as slippery as an eel.'

He called to the duty officer. 'See if you can get Dr Franks on the line, Dixon.' He went through to his own cubicle and waited, brooding on all the things he should have said to the psychologist and didn't, but would, by God! next time. Underneath, he was well aware that if thumbscrews were out, there was no way to force a man like Bottrell to talk except by flattering his vanity or knowing enough to lever out the truth.

The telephone bleeped. 'Franks? . . . Yes, it's me.'

'About my report?'

'No, about your friends, in particular about Dr James Bottrell.'

'I told you; I've never met the man.'

'But you know of him and you've corresponded. In any case it wouldn't matter if you'd never heard of him. I understand that he has a medical degree as well as a doctorate in psychology. In 1984 he was a consultant at the North Midlands Hospital—'

'Charles!' Franks interrupted. 'I wonder what your response would be if I asked you to get the dirt on the head of CID at Middleton-in-the-Marsh?'

'I doubt if Middleton-in-the-Marsh would have a CID

officer on the strength. In any case I'm not asking you for dirt, just about his professional standing and the appointments he's held.'

'Yes, and why he left them. No dirt, and you won't be interested. Anyway, I'll see what I can do but you'll owe me a good dinner if I come up with something.'

Wycliffe was thinking of Lizzie Biddick; her activities seemed confined to Duloe: her parents' home, her room in the big house, visits to Miller's cottage, and to James Bottrell's maisonette. Were these the true limits of her territory? Even the railway booking clerk had been struck by her naivety; conscious of her sense of adventure when she was merely buying a ticket for London. And what of Miller, and the quirky James? Whatever the breadth of their past experience it seemed that both had settled for life virtually within the confines of the estate. And Lander, and the Bottrells – did they venture far from their little promontory on the river?

He was reverting to his first impression of Duloe as a psychological island. But where, if anywhere, did it get him?

The Biddick girl. He couldn't get her out of his mind: culture from Miller, gin and sympathy from James Bottrell. And sex?

James had said something about her anxiety to be noticed, that she was busy constructing some private mythology through which she might come to terms with her insignificance.

But specialists specialize in half-truths. Wycliffe remembered his own youth: the feeling of being adrift, groping after those vague limits within which he must learn to live. He had been lucky, perhaps naturally cautious; too many are trapped in their own audacity. He hoped without much conviction that Lizzie hadn't paid with her life.

The clock above his table said, digitally, 16.15. That damned 24-hour clock! Another of the grudges he held, justly or unjustly, against the French.

There was a commotion in reception – DC Dixon expostulating, and Matt Biddick's voice, mumbling in sullen protest.

'Let him come in!'

The young man stood in the doorway of Wycliffe's cubicle, abashed now that he had attained his object.

'Sit down.'

Biddick perched himself on the edge of a bench seat. He reminded Wycliffe of a sturdy mongrel dog, ready to be friendly, but not to fawn. Wycliffe said: 'You went to the cottage with Mr Fox this morning? I haven't had his report yet.'

The boy shrugged. 'I couldn't help much. Only a couple of things. I remember the bottom drawer of his desk was full of stuff, now it's empty.'

'What did he keep there?'

'There was scores of letters – all in their envelopes like, but slit open. He must've saved 'em up for years.'

'You said there were two things.'

'Yes, his diary – a big thick exercise book, it was always in the top drawer. Whenever he couldn't remember something he would look it up in his diary. He used to say: "It's all here, Mattie, boy!" He used to call me that.'

The boy was blinking rapidly and there were tears between his lids. He pulled himself together. 'But that wasn't what I come about. I think I might've found something.'

'Tell me.'

'You know Lander's studio? . . . There's a well on the

rising ground behind there. The old couple who lived in the house used to get their water from it before Lander put the pipes in.'

'So?'

'Somebody's bin messing about with the cover. They've had it off and put it back. They've tried to make it look like it's never bin off but you can tell . . . It's a wood cover an' before it was all covered with grass and suchlike.'

Wycliffe got up from his chair. 'Let's take a look.'

In the adjoining cubicle DC Curnow was typing a report. Wycliffe recruited him. Curnow was blond, six feet-two and big with it, throwing doubt on his claim to unalloyed Cornish descent. His other distinguishing attribute was an insatiable thirst for knowledge. Folklore had it that he spent his spare time working through the *Encyclopaedia Britannica* and it was said that he had reached Volume Five: 'Conifer-Ear diseases.'

They passed through the white gate and crossed Lander's drive, apparently unobserved.

If Lizzie Biddick had met her death anywhere on the estate then her body would almost certainly be found in the immediate neighbourhood unless it had been removed by boat. Presumably that was possible, though the only available boat seemed to be the skiff in the boathouse.

They trooped down the narrow path through the trees and came in sight of the creek with the roof of the little house just below them. Biddick pointed to the left of the path, to somewhere in the featureless growth of nettles and brambles which covered the rising ground behind the house. 'In there.'

They followed him along a trail, recently trampled, and came to a small clearing. Grass and twigs had been strewn over a hinged wooden cover about thirty inches square. They were ten yards or so from the little house and level with the shuttered windows of the upper floor. A barely discernible path led to rough granite steps which descended to the backyard.

'All right, let's have the cover up.'

The debris was easily swept aside. It was obvious that the cover had been recently disturbed, the edges were free and rust had flaked from the hinges. Curnow lifted it with ease and laid it back.

The well was circular, lined with stone, and parged with clay below about five feet. The water level was ten feet or so lower than that. Just below it's dark gleaming surface Wycliffe could see what looked like the twin handles of a bag of some sort.

Biddick was staring down into the well, tense and silent.

Wycliffe spoke to break the spell: 'Have you any idea how deep it is?'

He was shaken but he made an effort. 'No. I remember it used to run dry in a drought – like now.' He added, after a pause: 'If we can rig a pulley and a rope sling I'll go down.'

Wycliffe laid a hand on his arm. 'Better not; leave it to us.'

That evening a small group gathered around the well: Wycliffe, Kersey, Fox with his camera, and a little man in overalls, a police technician who would do the work. The light had turned golden, the waters of the creek had a coppery hue, and the birds were silent. On these summer evenings by the river, the light, the stillness and the silence combine to engender a sense of foreboding, even of menace.

A uniformed policeman was stationed in Lander's drive to stop anyone coming down the path. Lander had been told of what was going on and his only comment had been: 'I'd forgotten there was a well.'

An aluminium ladder, assembled in sections, had been lowered into the well and secured by crooks at the top. Its lowest rung just reached the surface of the water.

Wycliffe said: 'Carry on.' The little man in overalls got his feet on the ladder and started to descend. He carried a short pole with a crook on the end, like a boat-hook. Though he was small and the ladder was placed vertically against the wall of the well, there was little room for manoeuvre. Standing on the bottom rung he fished with his hook and caught the handles at his first try. It was a bag, and heavy; he had to climb the ladder, dragging the bag after him. When he reached the top Kersey took it from him.

It was a large, blue canvas hold-all, filled so that it must have been difficult to run the zip. Tied to one handle was a label, sodden but still readable: 'Miss Lizzie Biddick, Passenger to Paddington'.

Kersey was moved; his own daughters were close to Lizzie's age. 'Poor little sod! You'd think she was off to Lapland but she went nowhere.'

He was stooping over the bag and he looked up at Wycliffe. 'Shall I open it?'

'Just to make sure.'

Fox was taking photographs for the record.

With difficulty Kersey drew the zip. The bag was stuffed with wet clothing. Kersey felt around inside and muttered: 'Just what it seems.'

Both men had been troubled by the image of a dismembered corpse.

The man in overalls said: 'Do you want me to have another go?'

He went down again, this time using his pole to feel around in the water. After a moment or two his voice came, echoing up the well: 'Something here, guv!'

'Careful.'

'I'm touching bottom, there's not much water . . . More mud than anything . . . I've got it!'

The hook came up with a second hold-all, similar to the first. It was dragged up the ladder and handed over to Kersey. Like the other, it contained nothing obviously sinister.

The little man was definite: 'There's nothing else down there of any size; that's for sure.'

Kersey said: 'You weren't expecting to find her down there.'

Wycliffe merely shook his head.

They had arrived too late for the evening meal. The landlady had offered to cook them something but they had settled for sandwiches and beer at one of the tables outside. Kersey was accepted as a boarder. 'If you're no more trouble than your boss I shan't complain.'

There were people at every table, mainly couples, some with children. It was dusk, there were gnats, and now and then a bat flitted silently forth and back above their heads, quartering the air.

Kersey said: 'So the search is on tomorrow.'

'You've fixed it?' Wycliffe's question seemed to arise more from politeness than interest.

'They've been very helpful – Reed's lot and division. We shall muster a team of eighteen or twenty, plus two dogs and their handlers. Reed is having sketch maps prepared and division are providing a couple of frogmen to look at the deep water around the quay and the boathouse.'

Wycliffe's thoughts were running on other lines; he said: 'The housekeeper thought she heard the girl returning to her room late at night—'

Kersey interrupted: 'But it was our joker, collecting her baggage, is that it?'

'It looks that way. He won't have left any traces but we'd better get Fox to look over the place first thing in the morning. Just to keep the record straight.'

Kersey yawned. 'Another?'

'No, I've had enough to make me sleep.'

'What's the programme for tomorrow?'

'I want you to supervise the search; I intend to spend some time with Lander, and I want Lucy available in the van.'

Lady Bottrell was watching television, one of those all-in wrestling contests between politicians which masquerade as informed discussion. It was evening, the french windows were still open, the courtyard was filled with golden light, and no breath of air stirred the leaves of the ash tree. The door opened and Lord Bottrell came in, agitated but hesitant, and stood looking at his wife.

'Are you watching that?'

She waved her electronic wand and the screen went blank. 'Obviously I'm not going to. What is it?'

'I've been talking to Harry Biddick. It seems they've opened the old well behind Tytreth and found Lizzie's bags – the things she was supposed to have taken with her.'

'Who opened the well?'

'The police – who do you think?'

Lady Bottrell looked pained. 'There is no need to lose your temper, Hugh. Have you spoken to Lander?'

He knew that his worries were about to be elucidated by a simple process of logic which would leave him feeling frustrated and inadequate.

'I tried, but Beth said he'd shut himself up in his study

and switched off his phone. She asked him but he wouldn't speak to me. It looks bad.'

'You think the Biddick girl is dead?'

'Evidently the police think so and so does poor Biddick. What else can anyone think? This, on top of Tony . . .' He was near to tears.

Lady Bottrell's smooth brow wrinkled into a frown. 'Tell me truthfully, Hugh, how far are you implicated in all this?'

He slumped on to the settee. 'I am not "implicated" as you call it! I am upset and worried.' He spread his hands in appeal. 'Who wouldn't be?'

'You had a row with Tony Miller on the night before he died—'

He was shaken. 'Who told you that?'

'What were you quarrelling about? Was it the girl?'

He had picked up a newspaper to keep himself in countenance, now he dropped it again. 'Why, for God's sake, should we quarrel about her?'

'Perhaps you were jealous because he was spending time with her.'

'But that is nonsense! Tony had no interest in women – not in that way.'

'So what was the quarrel about – who was it about?'

'It had nothing to do with anything that has happened – nothing!'

'Who?'

'The boy Biddick – Matthew.'

For the first time Lady Bottrell was taken by surprise and she was incredulous. 'You are telling me that Tony was having an affair with that young lout and that you demeaned yourself—' She broke off, unable to continue. 'Really, Hugh, you should write this up for the tabloids and pay off our debts.'

The door opened and James Bottrell came in. ‘Am I interrupting something?’

In a perfectly normal voice she said: ‘Of course not! Don’t be foolish, James.’

Chapter Nine

Next morning there was more activity at the entrance to Duloe than the cats had slept through since 1815 when Major General Lord Bottrell, Second Baron, returned home to a hero's welcome after Waterloo. The Incident Van was hemmed in by a police personnel carrier, a Land Rover, and a clutch of patrol and crime cars. A score of men and women, searchers to be, wearing working uniforms and wellington boots, milled about waiting for the briefing. Two German shepherd dogs sniffed and wagged and, very occasionally, yelped in the excitement of the moment. From the steps of the Incident Van Kersey called forth order out of chaos while Wycliffe remained inside, unseen.

'You all know what you are looking for. We want a thorough search, with a minimum of disturbance or damage. A young woman is missing and she must be found. We don't know what has happened to her but there are circumstances which suggest that she did not leave the area last Monday week as she intended to do.

'Sergeant Jarvis is in charge of the search; he will be stationed in his command vehicle in front of the big house and you will report to and take instructions from him.

'I am handing you over to Sergeant Jarvis.'

The searchers were paired off, instructions given, maps and beating sticks issued, emphasis was laid on co-ordination through radio and visual contact, and at 08.20

hours the searchers moved off. Already police frogmen were at work in and around the boathouse where there was a depth of water at all states of the tide.

Back in the van Kersey said to Wycliffe, 'I'll see the circus on the road then I'll be back.'

As Kersey was leaving the telephone bleeped. 'Wycliffe.'

'Dr Franks for you, sir.'

'About James Bottrell: you're in for a disappointment – no dirt to speak of. It seems he was a late starter academically; his limp is due to a tubercular knee-joint which blighted his childhood and messed up his education. Anyway, he eventually did his pre-clinical at Oxford and then went on to King's. After his hospital stint he joined a general practice in Nottingham – I'm short on dates but you'll have to put up with that. All I've got is that in '72 or '73 he was back at university for a post-graduate course in psychology, followed by a consultancy at the North Midland. Later he joined the Prison Department as a psychologist and packed it in when his aunt left him money. I wish I had a rich aunt.'

'What about him as a man?'

'You mean, what about the dirt. There isn't any. He has a reputation as a cold fish – very. Acquaintances, but no friends – he fended off colleagues when they wanted to be sociable. His treatments were sometimes unconventional but never over the line. As to sex, he seems to have had it off with any discreetly available female.' Franks ended: 'Is that worth a dinner?'

'No, but maybe I'll stretch a point.'

It was hot; the searchers were in for a gruelling day. The weathermen had predicted inland temperatures in the mid-eighties. Even at Duloe, on the river and within a mile or two of the open sea, there was no hint of a breeze. At ten o'clock Lucy Lane was in the van catching up on paper work – word processing, chasing her fingers over the keyboard like a frenetic virtuoso playing Scarlatti.

In his own cubicle, Wycliffe, in shirt sleeves, flicked a ballpoint in and out, staring out of the window at a squirrel half-way up a tree. The squirrel seemed to return his gaze so that he was persuaded the creature could see him despite the one-way glass. The boisterous arrival of a gunmetal BMW, sleek and stylish, startled them both.

The driver was a woman: late-thirties, blonde; wearing tailored mauve trousers with a matching, patterned, silk blouse. Her figure was slim, her hair sculptured to her head; she had jade earrings, and an air of elegance. The car door slammed and, almost at once, she was confronting Potter, the duty officer. 'Chief Superintendent Wycliffe, please.'

Potter would have prevaricated but she cut him short. 'Tell him I am Tony Miller's sister.'

Wycliffe put on his jacket and went to meet her; she held out her hand. It was cool, his was sweaty.

'Olivia Sanders, née Ross.'

She put down her suede handbag and took a seat across the table from Wycliffe, at ease with all sorts and conditions of men.

For some reason a conventional expression of sympathy seemed out of place so he did not attempt one. 'I assume you have been to the police station?' (If she had and he hadn't been told there would be trouble.)

'No. I spent the night in Truro, made a few enquiries, and learned that I should probably find you here.' She smiled. 'I wanted to be sure of reaching the top.'

Wycliffe was annoyed that the woman made him feel he had something to live up to. 'I expect you know that your brother died on Sunday night but you may not have known at first that he had changed his name.'

'I did know, as a matter of fact. That is partly what

I've come to tell you, but before I do you should know something of the family. Tony and I were the only children and I am the elder by two years. Our father was a drunk – amiable to outsiders, less so at home.'

She had prepared her little speech, succinct and convincing; now she was delivering it with as little emotion as if it concerned people with whom she had only a professional connection.

'Fortunately mother made sure that we had a reasonable education. I became a nurse and as soon as it was practicable I left home and never went back. I qualified, and eventually came south to work in Dorchester General. I kept in touch with my brother – birthdays, Christmas – that sort of thing, then, one day, to my astonishment, he turned up in Dorchester, married, with a job in the Parks Department. His wife was sixteen years older, and a bitch.'

She paused and looked straight at Wycliffe. 'I expect you know the upshot of that little romance. Tony went to prison, we lost contact, and I heard no more of him until just over a fortnight ago when he telephoned me from the Crown and I had a meal with him there. It was then that he told me he had changed his name.'

Wycliffe was gazing out of the window at the BMW and her eyes followed his. 'You are wondering how the BMW fits in with Health Service nursing. It doesn't. For me things have changed. I'm now a partner in, and matron of, a private nursing home.' Another smile. 'But in any case that is my husband's car – you see, in a traditional hospital romance, I married the surgical consultant. He's a neurologist.'

Wycliffe decided to be bored; he turned to look at her with mild, dreamy eyes. 'I still don't understand why it has taken you four days to make any contact.'

She rested her hands on the table, fingering the

bracelet of her watch. 'I admit it must seem a little strange. The fact is that my husband has rather rigid ideas about certain things.'

'He doesn't want you to become involved, is that it?'

'He doesn't even know that I met Tony and I certainly don't want him to know that I have contacted you now. As far as he is concerned I have no longer any connection with my family. That is what I came to tell you.'

'And the car?'

'Bernard – my husband – is away, attending a symposium in London. He always travels any distance by train and the BMW is a great improvement on my workhorse Escort . . .'

'Why did your brother want to renew contact?'

'I'm not sure; I think he wanted me to lend him money. He didn't ask outright but he went into some detail about a scheme he had for starting a business – landscape gardening, that sort of thing. He even talked about the amount of capital he would need.'

'So you had the definite impression that he intended to leave his job here?'

'Oh, he made no bones about that! He said the situation was becoming intolerable.'

'In what way?'

She made a helpless gesture. 'Tony's emotional life has always tended towards the dramatic. This time it was some homosexual entanglement from which he wanted to extricate himself but the other party wouldn't let go. It seems things had reached crisis point with recriminations and threats making life very uncomfortable.'

'Did he name the other party?'

'No.'

'Hasn't it occurred to you that this relationship might have provided the motive for his murder?'

She looked at him, her hard, blue eyes incredulous.

'You think that's possible? I'm afraid I didn't take it very seriously and I can't really believe—'

'Did you lead him to think that you might help him financially?'

'I did not. I suggested that he talked to his bank. I owe a great deal to my husband and however unwarranted his prejudice may be, I would do nothing to seriously displease him.'

'You are referring to his attitude towards homosexuality?'

'Of course!'

'Isn't such a prejudice unusual in a medical man and a neurologist at that?'

'Perhaps you are confusing neurology with psychology.'

Wycliffe felt snubbed, an unusual experience which was probably good for him.

'Are you the next of kin?'

'No; father is still alive. You didn't know?'

'We found nothing in your brother's possession to indicate any relative.'

'I'll give you his address.' She took a professional card from her handbag and wrote on the back. 'When I last heard, he was still more or less compos mentis . . . He's in some kind of sheltered accommodation for the elderly.'

What she had told him was helpful; he now had a reasonable explanation of Miller's visit to Dorchester and of his depression. More important, he had a hint of another side to the quarrel with Lord Bottrell on the night before the murder.

Wycliffe found it possible to be moderately pleased with the woman; he even thanked her for coming.

'If my name can be kept out . . .'

But that was pushing her luck. 'I can promise nothing at this stage.'

She picked up her handbag. 'If I could see where Tony lived . . . ?'

She had every right. He called Lucy Lane and introduced the two women, fascinated by the ensuing mutual appraisal. As they walked away from the van he heard the woman say: 'So you are a detective sergeant . . .'

He had disliked her. Of course she had put on an act, everybody does, but hers had offended him because it was blatant. An act, to be acceptable, must be so well practised that it fits like a glove. But is it then any longer an act?

There was a tap on his door and Potter, the duty officer, came in. 'Radio message from PC Fuller, sir. Subject has just gone down the path to Tytreth.'

On the pretext of fending off sightseers and the press Wycliffe had stationed a man in Lander's drive with instructions to report the lawyer's movements. Although it was past ten o'clock his car was still parked in front of the house; he had not gone to his office. Wycliffe had hoped that for one reason or another he would be drawn to his little house by the creek so that the inevitable interview – confrontation? – could take place there. He liked to meet any important witness at least once in their preferred habitat; talking to anybody in a police interview room is like studying animal behaviour in a laboratory.

He said to Potter: 'Tell Mr Kersey I shall be at Tytreth.'

Walking down the path through the trees he saw none of the searchers but he heard an occasional shout and once a dog barked. As he came in sight of the back of the house he saw that the shutters of one of the upstairs windows had been opened and, dimly, through the small window panes, he could see into the room. Lander was there, his gangling figure bent over something which he seemed to be polishing with some vigour.

He went down the steps and around to the front door. The padlock had been removed but the door was shut and there was no knocker or bell. To save his knuckles he rapped on the door with a coin. Almost at once he heard footsteps on the stairs, a bolt was drawn and the door opened. Lander was in his shirt sleeves, wearing a grey apron and, in a rubber-gloved hand, he held a piece of rag. Wycliffe noticed a faint smell of turpentine.

Lander seemed startled. 'Wycliffe!' He immediately controlled himself. 'You took me by surprise; no-one ever comes here.'

'May I come in?'

The door opened into a tiny lobby and Wycliffe followed Lander through a second door into a room lit only by artificial light. It must have been the former kitchen-cum-living-room but now it was a photographic laboratory though, even to Wycliffe, it looked old fashioned. There was a sink set in a bench with an impressive array of bottles and jars on shelves above it. There was some chemical glassware, and a stack of white enamel trays of different sizes. The only item which struck Wycliffe as typical of a modern darkroom was an enlarger, draped under polythene in one corner. Stairs led to the upper floor. Overall there was that faintly acrid smell associated with any stock of chemicals.

Lander was manifestly uneasy and inclined to aggression. He peeled off the glove he was wearing and tossed it, with the rag, into the sink. 'I suppose you know that photography is my hobby.' He added: 'You'd better come through.'

They moved into the adjoining room which, until Lander opened the shutters, was in almost total darkness. The transformation from darkness to brilliant sunshine from the creek was dramatic. The room, formerly the parlour, was large and Lander had made it his studio. One wall was taken up by a nest of metal drawers of various sizes, presumably for his collection of photographs and, above them, were bookshelves. In the middle of the room a massive camera stood on a tripod, all teak and gleaming brass. For the rest there were numerous lamps on telescopic stands, various screens and a low bench with padded drapes which could have served as a model's throne.

'Please sit down.'

Lander, himself, sat in one of the two armchairs and placed the tips of his bony fingers together, rigid and expectant. The previous evening he had been flushed by whisky; now he looked grey, either a sick or a very worried man.

Wycliffe was relaxed and conversational, anxious not to raise the tension too soon. 'This is a very pleasant room. Do you spend much time here?'

'All the time I can spare.' There was a brief pause while the lawyer sought for something to match the mood: 'Somebody said: "If you're going to have a past you need a house to keep it in."'

'And this is your past?'

A faint smile. 'Also, I hope, my future.'

'Devoted to photography.'

'To historical aspects of photography. The modern obsession, clicking away with a contrivance of high-tech gadgetry, has no appeal.'

'Judging from the equipment next door you do all your own processing.'

Lander was responding to Wycliffe's approach. He leaned forward in his chair, crossed his legs, and clasped his long fingers about his knees. 'You probably wonder what goes on out there. I admit that it's more like an alchemist's kitchen than a photographer's darkroom. Actually I try to repeat the techniques of the early photographers using their materials. I've tried my hand at daguerreotypes, calotypes, wet and dry plate work . . . As a youngster I wanted to be a chemist, just as my father before me had wanted to be an architect, but tradition was too strong.'

He was talking too much.

Wycliffe turned to the museum-piece camera, bringing the subject back to photography. 'Do you use this monster or is it merely an interesting fossil?'

'I use it constantly. I call it my Old Faithful.'

It was strange to see a reflex softening of those bizarre features at the mere mention of the camera. Despite long experience of the masks people wear Wycliffe could still be surprised by a chameleon-like change triggered by an object or a phrase.

'It was about a photograph that I came to see you.'

From his wallet Wycliffe produced the defaced print of the nude girl and handed it over. It was obvious that Lander had braced himself for whatever might come and the mask was once more in place, but as he held the photograph his hand trembled.

After an interval he said in a controlled, formal voice: 'This is a Nadar print – that is to say it was made by the Frenchman, Gaspard-Felix Tournochon, who adopted "Nadar" as his pseudonym. He did a number of nude studies – daring for their time – in the sixties and seventies of the last century. May I ask how you came by it?'

'It was sent to me anonymously through the mail.'

'And you are obviously taking it seriously. Couldn't it be a sick joke?'

Wycliffe was patient. 'I am taking it seriously because it was posted in the Truro district during the weekend in which Miller was killed and the pendant which has been drawn around the girl's neck is identical with a birth-sign pendant worn by Lizzie Biddick.'

Lander handed back the photograph. He was cautious, vetting his every word, but his hand was unsteady. 'I see! As far as I knew, until last night, she had left for London more than a week ago.'

'And it is more than a week ago – the evening of last Sunday week – that she was seen by Mrs Christophers, leaving the house, and by Dr Bottrell whom she called on to say goodbye. No-one admits to having seen her since. Her rail ticket, her money, and other personal things have been found in her room; her bags, already packed, have been retrieved from your well, and we are now searching the neighbourhood for her body.'

The lawyer was grave. 'I can understand your concern, but the photograph—'

Wycliffe cut in: 'I am anxious to trace the source of the photograph. I suppose Nadar prints are not easily come by?'

'No, but any serious collector might have some; I have two or three in my collection.'

'But not one of this particular print?'

Lander subjected him to his sombre gaze before replying: 'No, I have never seen that particular print or another like it.'

There was a pause, as though a certain stage had been reached at which their relative positions were defined.

Twice, the lawyer's thin lips parted as though he would speak but he remained silent. Wycliffe appeared to brood over the print then, abruptly, he held it up. 'Would you agree that this was intended to draw my attention to Lizzie Biddick's disappearance?'

Lander considered the point. 'If the pendant is taken

to identify the girl then I suppose that must have been the intention.'

'And to suggest that she had been murdered?'

'That seems to follow.'

'One would have thought it simpler to send an anonymous letter but if a photograph was used, why not a modern one? Why deface a print which had some value and must have been difficult to come by?'

Lander made a dismissive gesture. 'Your correspondent – if one may call him that – must be a very devious individual.'

He sat in his chair, doing his best to appear impassive, his great jaw set, his brown eyes fixed on Wycliffe in an unblinking stare.

By contrast Wycliffe's eyes were vague, his expression dreamy, and his manner tentative. 'Hasn't it occurred to you that this may have been a deliberate attempt to implicate you? The print was posted locally and you are well known as a photographer and collector of historic photographs. As I see it my attention is being directed to a possible link between you and the missing girl.'

Lander was showing signs of increasing uneasiness, the long bony fingers of his right hand began to beat out a tattoo on the arm of his chair. He said, with emphasis: 'Mr Wycliffe, I know that girl only as the daughter of Lord Bottrell's gardener and as a housemaid at Duloe.'

'She has never been inside this house?'

'Not, at least, since it has been occupied by me.'

Looking past the lawyer, out of the window, Wycliffe could see the still waters of the creek, the moored boats, and the toy-town houses on the other side. He had one of those moments of self-doubt, of incredulity; finding it surprising that he, Charlie Wycliffe, should be here in this strange room, interrogating a man he scarcely knew, trying to extract an admission which might make that man a murder suspect.

Lander was looking at him with a curious expression; he appeared to be waiting. With an effort Wycliffe recovered his role and his voice became official: 'I think, sir, that you should be clear about the situation: this is likely to become a murder inquiry in the near future and I must point out that reticence, understandable in ordinary circumstances, could be misconstrued now.'

The lawyer was shaken. 'Are you threatening me, Chief Superintendent?'

'I am asking you to bear in mind that there are people in whom Lizzie Biddick confided. I have been told of certain photographs which she claimed you have here. I am not suggesting that their possession in any way infringes the law, merely making the point that the girl seems to have been familiar with this place. Add to that the fact that her baggage has been found in a well behind the house and I have reasonable grounds for a more detailed investigation.'

The point went home but Lander fought back. His manner was mildly contemptuous: 'I hardly think I need take seriously a statement about the contents of this house which must have reached you at second-hand. It is no more than gossip. As to the discovery of the girl's baggage, it is obvious that the well was a convenient place to dump things, the possession of which would have been incriminating. That the well happens to be on my land is irrelevant.'

Wycliffe was unruffled. 'You may be right, but in a case which looks more and more like murder I must follow every lead however slender.'

Lander was agitated, he placed the tips of his fingers together and it seemed to steady him. 'How do you propose to follow this "lead" as you call it?'

'I was about to ask you to allow my men to make a search of these premises as a matter of routine.'

Lander contrived to look astonished. 'With what object?'

'To confirm your statement that Lizzie Biddick did not come here.'

'And if I refuse?'

'I am sure that you will not be uncooperative, but a refusal would force me to apply for a warrant.'

'You mean you would go to a magistrate?'

'Certainly.'

Lander made no response but there was a faint visible pulse in his left temple.

Wycliffe said nothing and for a time there was silence in the sunlit room. Distantly the clock in the village church chimed and struck twelve; it seemed to take for ever. The tide had uncovered the muddy margins of the shore and several of the smaller craft across the creek were aground.

Abruptly, Lander broke the silence. 'I have nothing to hide as far as the law is concerned and I want it clearly understood that I know nothing of the girl's whereabouts nor of what happened to her. As far as I knew she had left for London as she intended.'

Wycliffe, speaking softly, said: 'But she did come here from time to time?'

Lander nodded. 'Yes.'

'A regular visitor?'

'Most Sundays. I was probably foolish to deny it in the first place but one tries to avoid domestic friction.'

'You agree to your premises being searched?'

He reacted angrily: 'Do you think I want you applying for a warrant? Even if you didn't get it the application and the fact that I had refused permission would discredit me professionally – as you well know.'

'You will let me have the keys of this place until a search can be arranged?'

'Do I have a choice?'

Wycliffe retained his official manner. 'You realize that I must also ask you to make a formal statement concerning your association with the girl? You have not been officially interrogated, there has been no witness to our conversation and nothing has been recorded. You may come to the Incident Van or, if you prefer, to Truro police station.'

'I will come to your van. I want you to understand that I am most concerned to avoid publicity which could damage me professionally and in my family life.'

Wycliffe was left with a sense of wonder at the spectacle of a man like Lander, a lawyer, putting his reputation into the hands of a young girl; making himself dependent on her goodwill and her discretion, or on his ability to buy both. The sergeant under whom Wycliffe had served his green years had once remarked: 'There is commonsense, there is professional caution, there is decency, and there is the marriage tie, but there is also Sex.'

On the face of it Lizzie's demands had been modest, but perhaps not, and thereby a tale might hang.

On his way to lunch Wycliffe called in at the Incident Van. There were two reports. The first was brief, on the examination of Miller's car. Nothing had been found to suggest that the missing girl had been a passenger in it, voluntarily or otherwise. The second report included an inventory of the contents of Lizzie Biddick's two hold-alls, recovered from the well. Clothing accessories and toilet articles accounted for the great bulk of items but among the rest there were several paperbacks, a couple of magazines and one item that was starred:

'Item 28: A4 envelope containing 14 photographs; various subjects and sizes.' A footnote read: 'These photographs are included with this inventory as they may have interest.'

Somebody showing a bit of initiative. Wycliffe tipped out the photographs. Despite immersion the envelope itself was only slightly damp and the photographs were untouched. He recognized several snapshots of members of the Biddick family, they were labelled on the back with first name diminutives, or 'Mum' and 'Dad'. Of the others there was one of Miller, seated in front of his cottage.

One photograph stood out from the rest; it was larger, and an obvious quality product. It showed Lizzie herself, quite naked, in a pose identical with that of the girl in the Nadar print. On the back was written: 'Guess who?'

Thoughtful, Wycliffe walked to the pub to share the table in the alcove (now carrying a 'Reserved' card) with Lucy Lane. Tourists crowded the dining-room and clustered around the bar. There was an extra waitress on duty but the landlady herself came over.

She spoke in a low voice: 'I've got a bit of fresh salmon, if you fancy it – with a nice salad; and for a sweet there's a bread pudding in the oven – my own recipe. Don't worry! It won't lie heavy on your stomach, 'tis light as a feather.'

'With a half-bottle of something light and fruity it sounds wonderful.'

Lucy said: 'Mr Kersey not coming?'

Wycliffe explained. 'How did it go with Olivia Sanders née Ross?'

Lucy took her time. 'At least she's the sort of woman I can get on with – a realist. What she had to say about her brother was interesting. She thinks he should have been a creative artist of some sort but he was too mentally lazy to discipline himself. While he was still at school he had poems published and he played in the regional Youth Orchestra, but when it came to further education it was easier to drift into the local garage. Of course his father didn't help.'

The salmon arrived with a salad which was a good deal more imaginative than the usual tomato, limp lettuce leaf, and onion ring which masquerade as salad in most pubs. And the half-bottle was a hock, not at all bad.

'According to his sister, Miller had a real guilt complex about his homosexuality and the woman he married made the most of it.'

Wycliffe poured the wine. 'Lander is coming in to make a formal statement about his relations with Lizzie and I'm turning Fox loose in his studio.'

Lucy dissected the salmon, speared a little of the salad on her fork, and popped it into her mouth. Wycliffe always felt loutish when eating in her company. Having cleared her mouth, she sipped her wine and patted her lips. 'You think he killed her?'

'It's possible, I suppose.' He was casual.

'And Miller was killed because he knew too much.'

Wycliffe sipped his wine and said nothing for a while; then: 'All crimes of violence are distressing but here, it seems to me, there is a chilling element, calculating . . . passionless.'

Lucy Lane looked at him in surprise. 'You think so?'

He had picked up his knife and fork but dropped them again. 'What I think is that we need to get a fresh hold.' He was looking at her with his most solemn and stolid expression.

Chapter Ten

'They've found her, sir!' Potter, the duty officer, with a rare display of animation.

'Where?'

'Block twenty-five on the grid, sir.'

Pinned to the display board was a copy of the map supplied to the searchers. It had been divided into a grid of fifty-metre squares. Wycliffe studied the map. Block twenty-five covered part of the shore of the upper creek adjacent to Lander's studio.

'Mr Kersey was here when word came through and he arranged for scenes-of-crime and the doc to attend. He's down there now, himself.'

'Then I'll join him.'

The suspicion of a grin flickered across Potter's thick lips betraying his thought: 'No show without Punch'. Chief supers are not expected to be where the action is except in times of dire emergency.

The path from Lander's drive, down through the trees to the Upper Creek, was now familiar ground. He scarcely noticed his surroundings and had no eyes for the view. When he reached the strand the house was as he had first seen it, blind and deserted; Fox had not yet started work on the lawyer's hide-away. Wycliffe was surprised to find no-one about, then he heard voices not far away and a constable appeared on the path which led in the direction of the boathouse and the quay.

'This way, sir.' Potter had lost no time in warning his comrades.

Kersey and three or four of the searchers were close by, screened from the house by a scrub of elder, blackthorn, gorse and bramble. They were on the little promontory where he had seen signs of a former industry; that industry, he had discovered since, was boatbuilding in the early years of the century.

Kersey was brooding over a ditch – a channel less than eighteen inches wide and about the same in depth, cut for some purpose now unknown.

The girl was lying face upwards in the ditch and she was naked, even her birth-sign pendant had been removed. Her body was bloated and discoloured; she had been dead for several days.

And there were the tell-tale signs of a particular kind of violence: bruises on either side of and slightly below the larynx, more bruising around the neck; petechiae about the face, neck and chest; cyanosis . . . She had been throttled.

Kersey said: 'We saw the dotty picture; now we've got the real thing. Poor little bastard! . . . One of the dogs found her; you can't see this ditch until you're nearly in it.' He pointed to a couple of rotting planks lying nearby. 'They were on top of her, weighed down by stones.'

'To keep the gulls off.'

'I suppose so; they would soon have given the game away with their squawking.'

Even now three or four herring gulls planed and swooped overhead as though waiting their chance. The girl was lying on a bed of black estuarine mud and her flesh, although protected by the planks from the gulls, had been ravaged by the more surreptitious attentions of crustaceans.

Kersey had briefed himself from local knowledge.

'They tell me there's more than a foot of water in this channel at an average high tide – enough to submerge the body.'

'But not to move it.'

'No, the weighted planks made sure she stayed where she was put.'

When Wycliffe was able to turn his attention to the surroundings he was surprised to find that they were not overlooked. The scrub bushes and trees which shielded them from the house also cut them off from the creek and the river. A very private place for murder. But had the girl been killed on the spot? Or had her body been dragged or carried from elsewhere? The ground, stony in any case, was now parched and hard so that whatever had been done it was unlikely that any traces would be found.

Fox arrived to take photographs and to plot the exact position of the body on the map. He was followed by the local doctor, a young man, somewhat awed by the task which had been thrust upon him. He introduced himself: 'Dr Prentiss . . .' and broke off as he caught sight of the body. 'Good God! How long has she been there?'

'Up to eleven days. No-one admits to having seen her in that time – a week last Sunday.'

Prentiss was thoughtful. 'So that, alternately, she must have been lying in salt water, or left high, if not dry, according to the state of the tide. The ambient temperature will have fluctuated wildly between the extremes when she was submerged at night and exposed to full sun at low tide by day – with every possible variation in between.'

The doctor was setting his mental house in order to good effect. He ran a hand through his mop of blond curls. 'What exactly are you expecting me to tell you?'

Wycliffe was understanding. 'To be frank, not much. In the circumstances I doubt if the pathologist will be very informative before he's done the autopsy.'

Confidence restored, the young man went on: 'She obviously didn't drown, she was strangled – or throttled. There are no other obvious signs of ill-treatment but it may be a different story when she's out of there and one is able to take a good look. I assume she's the missing girl?'

Kersey said: 'We are assuming that too, but even her mother would have difficulty in recognizing her.'

Her mother – Wycliffe thought of the vigorous and resolute little matriarch and her brood. Abruptly, the thing in the ditch became the girl who, searching for a way of escape, had blundered against the glass walls of her cage like a frenetic bumblebee. Wycliffe felt anger rise within him; it was unprofessional and unproductive but healthy, even in a policeman.

To Kersey he said: 'You'd better notify the coroner and Dr Franks.' He looked up and was shaken to see Matt Biddick coming along the path from the direction of the quay.

He hurried to meet him. There was no need to say anything: the boy said it for him: 'You've found her.'

'Yes.'

'How did she . . . ?'

'I don't know yet. As soon as I do . . .'

'Can I see her?'

'Better not.'

A momentary show of temper, quickly followed by resignation.

Wycliffe said: 'I'm going to tell your mother now.'

The boy put out his hand. 'No! I'll tell mother.'

They were waiting for the mortuary van – rather for the men who manned it; the van could get no closer than the Landers' drive.

Wycliffe looked about him: nothing had changed. Why should it? Nature was taking its course, part of the recycling process. Humans made such a fuss; and there were far too many of them anyway. That was the logic of life. But compassion and fear blend with human perversity to defy all logic, and Wycliffe was moved by a sense of strangeness, of alienation, as well as by the pathos of it all.

Two attendants from the mortuary arrived, piloted by a uniformed man. They brought a stretcher and a polythene envelope in which the body would be placed.

Straps were manoeuvred under the girl, she was lifted out of the ditch, and, within minutes, all that remained of Lizzie Biddick had been carried away.

Suddenly Wycliffe felt very tired; there was a sense of anticlimax – strange in the circumstances – but he had experienced it before. They trooped back to the Incident Van, the stretchers were recalled and sent on their way; the two frogmen had packed their gear and departed long since. Wycliffe made a brief statement to the press who had monitored the search after their own fashion.

Now the congestion outside the gates of Duloe was reduced to the Incident Van and a couple of crime cars.

Wycliffe, slumped in his chair, said: 'We still haven't found the clothes she was wearing when she set out that Sunday night.'

They were in luck with the post mortem. Dr Franks was available and, by six o'clock, less than four hours after the finding of the body, he was on the telephone to Wycliffe.

'For your ears only. I've made no internal examination so this is provisional, but it's pretty obvious that she was throttled. I can find no evidence of sexual intercourse having taken place at or around the time of her death but I wouldn't expect to when she's been lying in a ditch, washed by the tide, for God knows how long. So, on the face of it, a common-or-garden sex crime.'

Wycliffe said: 'We worked that out for ourselves.'

'Then you were wrong. Admittedly it could still be a sex crime but with an unusual variation. Somebody coshed her first. Nothing fancy, just a good old fashioned swipe with a sock full of sand or similar.'

'Enough to kill outright?'

'Obviously not, because it wasn't what she died of. But enough to put her out and endanger life. There may well be a fracture of the occiput and possibly contrecoup lesions, but I shan't know yet. More on that in our next. But going back to the throttling: the killer seems to have made deliberate use of some necklace thing she was wearing to render the pressure of his thumbs more effective. The nature of the bruising makes that pretty certain. I suppose he removed whatever it was, scared of possible prints.'

'So that's it then?'

'For the moment anyway. If I find later that she's been injected with Bulgarian umbrella poison I'll let you know.'

Wycliffe thanked him, and meant it. Not all pathologists are willing to raise their heads above their stainless steel sluices until they've prepared the ground with a barrage of typescript.

Wycliffe contacted headquarters, heading off some of the inevitable pressure from the media by arranging that future statements would be issued through a press officer at sub-division. He, himself, would attend a briefing following any significant development. The media was asked to avoid the vicinity of the estate. It wouldn't work altogether, but it might help.

When told of the pathologist's report, even Kersey admitted to some mystification. 'Odd! I suppose he coshed her because she struggled.'

'Having come provided with a suitable weapon.'

Wycliffe was sarcastic. 'I think Franks, by talking about a sand-filled sock, means a weapon with a certain resilience which can do a lot of damage without spilling blood and brains all over the place. These things don't lie around, waiting to come in handy.'

Kersey's rubbery features achieved one of his famous grimaces indicative of thought. 'I suppose he could have topped her because she threatened him, then tried to make it look like a sex crime.'

'Who, in this scenario, is he?'

'Lander, of course. Who else?'

'And what was she threatening Lander with?' Wycliffe's manner was irritatingly pedantic, usually a sign that he was groping after some idea of his own and was being confused by discussion. He went on: 'I admit that her passbook shows she was getting money from somebody – perhaps from Lander. Conceivably she was blackmailing him with the threat that she would make their association public; in which case, keeping her quiet might have been worth a few hundreds. But murder . . . ?'

For once Lucy aligned herself with Kersey. 'But we don't know, sir, what else she may have had on Lander. We've heard about dirty pictures but there could have been something really serious.'

Wycliffe nodded. 'All right, so let's assume that Lander thought he had reason to fear her – reason enough to kill her, would he have done it on his own doorstep? Would he have taken the trouble to collect her baggage, only to hide it down his own well?'

Kersey said: 'A sudden outburst of violence followed by blind panic. We've seen it often enough before.'

'An outburst of violence, with a cosh at the ready – which is where we came in. Let's leave it at that until Lander has said his piece; he's due to make a statement anyway. And first thing in the morning Fox can get back to the studio and find out what that has to tell us.'

Wycliffe leaned back in his chair and yawned. 'Meantime we've got a few – a very few, facts: the housekeeper says she saw Lizzie leaving the house at about half-past nine on the night she disappeared. James Bottrell says she was with him, "coming up for ten". Lander says he was expecting her at ten but that she didn't turn up. After that – nothing.'

Wycliffe suppressed another yawn. 'Nothing, that is, until now – an interval of eleven days. And during those eleven days Miller was murdered. It would be incredible if the two crimes were unconnected, yet there was a week between them. Of course, Miller was away for some of that time . . .'

'She came most Sundays, after she had helped with the meal at the house.'

'When did these visits start?'

'About a year ago.'

Lander was sitting opposite Wycliffe in the Incident Van with only the bench-like table and a cassette recorder between them. A uniformed constable stood by the door. Lander seemed distrait, he looked about him uncertainly as though not quite sure where he was, his eyes and his hands were never still.

'How did it start?'

'What? Oh, I met her when I was out walking the dog. She told me she was interested in photography . . .' His voice trailed off.

'What happened then?'

He looked at Wycliffe as though startled by the question then recollected himself. 'She asked me if I would recommend a reliable camera which wasn't too expensive. I was short with her at first but she seemed genuinely interested.'

'Did you suggest that she might come to the studio and talk it over?'

He frowned. 'I suppose I did; I don't know. Anyhow, she came. And now she's dead!' His eyes sought Wycliffe's, their expression haunted and oddly disturbing.

Wycliffe said: 'Mr Lander, you are making a statement in connection with two very serious crimes; you have been offered the chance to defer your statement until the morning when you may be more composed. I advise you, once more, to do that.'

The lawyer became very tense, the muscles of his great jaw tightened and colour showed in his pale cheeks. Speaking slowly, and enunciating each word with exaggerated clarity, he said: 'And I want this over – tonight!'

A moment later he added in a more normal voice: 'I will try to be more restrained but there is something you must understand: I needed Lizzie – I never in my life had a truly intimate relationship with any woman . . .' His voice let him down; his hands were trembling and he clasped them together. 'I would have done anything for Lizzie!'

Like a boy with his first girl, even the repetition of her name seemed to give him pleasure.

'The idea that I would have harmed her is . . . is preposterous! . . . Of course, you are sneering; any normal man would. I don't hold it against you.'

'I am not sneering, Mr Lander, far from it. I am trying to establish a sequence of events. Now, did Lizzie, at any time, ask you for money?'

'No, but after I'd known her a little while I made her a present.'

'How much?'

'Two hundred pounds, and I gave her other presents at intervals.' He was quieter, his outburst seemed to have calmed him.

'How much, over the year?'

'I don't know, perhaps a thousand.'

'Did she ever threaten you or demand anything else?'

'Never!'

There was a longish pause during which the tape could have picked up only background sounds from the police radio in the next compartment. Then, Wycliffe asked: 'When was the last time you saw her?'

In a voice that was barely audible he said: 'I saw her when I called on the Bottrells on Saturday evening – just briefly – in the corridor . . . She smiled at me.'

'You did not see her on the Sunday?'

'I didn't; I expected that she would come at about ten, but she did not.'

'You had an appointment?'

'An arrangement – like other Sundays, except that she wouldn't be staying the night.'

'You knew that she was off to London the following day?'

'I knew that was what she intended to do.'

'So this would have been a farewell visit.'

There was another lengthy silence, then, looking down at his hands, and speaking very quietly, he said: 'I was going to try to persuade her to stay.'

'How?'

Wycliffe could scarcely catch the words of his reply. 'I would have given her a choice.'

'A choice?'

'If she agreed to stay I would have given her a large sum of money.'

'Or?'

Without raising his eyes, he said: 'I would divorce my wife and marry her.' He leaned forward and clasped his hands tightly together on the table.

'The following day, when you heard that she had

gone, you must have been very distressed.'

'I couldn't believe that she would do that to me!' And after a pause, he added with curiously naive satisfaction: 'And she didn't, did she?'

'But you made no enquiries?'

His look was accusing. 'How could I? I hoped and expected that she would write, or telephone.'

The clock on the wall showed 20.25. The sun, close to setting, was screened by the trees and dusk had already settled over the little enclave of the cats.

The policeman by the door, shuffled his feet and coughed. Lander turned sharply; startled.

Wycliffe's manner became more official; his voice hardened: 'But we know now what happened to her, and her body was found in a ditch less than a hundred yards from your studio; her baggage was hidden in your well.'

Lander looked at him like a man under torture; but suffering roused him. He raised his voice: 'How *can* I say anything, when I know nothing?'

Wycliffe sat back in his chair. 'I have only one more question to ask you at this stage; then I am going to adjourn this interview: Did the photograph you saw – the Nadar print – come from your collection?'

Lander drummed his fingers on the table top then, abruptly, he said: 'I gave it to Lizzie.'

'Why?'

There was a far away look in his eyes. 'Lizzie spent a lot of time going through my collection. The photographs seemed to fascinate her – that one in particular. She said the girl was like her and she asked me to take one of her in the same pose.'

'And did you?'

He nodded.

'Please answer for the tape.'

'I did.'

'This interview ends at 20.35.' Wycliffe switched off the tape and turned again to Lander who sat, as though mesmerized. 'I may have further questions and it would be convenient if you did not go to your office in the morning.'

'Is that an instruction?'

'As you well know, Mr Lander, it is a request.'

That evening when Wycliffe called on the Biddicks to express his sympathy the whole family was gathered in the living-room to hear what he had to say. Lizzie's mother, dry-eyed but very pale, when asked if she really wanted the younger ones to hear how Lizzie died, was unequivocal: 'Lizzie was their sister; they've got the right.'

And her husband, like a well trained chorus, murmured: 'We're a family, Mr Wycliffe . . . A family . . .'

Wycliffe told them briefly what he had learned so far, and ended: 'One thing is certain; Lizzie didn't suffer. The blow would have meant immediate loss of consciousness.'

It was a strange experience; he was the centre of solemn and dignified attention from eight pairs of brown eyes, from the little girl on her mother's lap to Harry Biddick who sat, his unlit pipe clenched between his teeth.

The boy, Matt, was the first to speak. 'Did it happen where she was found?'

'I can't say at the moment. I hope that we shall know more later and I can promise that you will be told everything.'

Matt would have been more pressing but his mother cut in: 'No more, now, Matt! I reckon Mr Wycliffe has been straight with us and he's not going to be asked a lot of questions he can't answer.'

Wycliffe came away, deeply impressed, knowing that this experience would remain with him as one of the most moving of his professional life.

Before going to bed he telephoned his wife.

'It's me . . .' The usual ritual.

'Are you coming home?'

'Not yet.' He hesitated, not having formulated in his mind the question he most wanted answered. 'No news at your end?'

'Nothing in particular. Ruth telephoned earlier.'

'Is she all right?'

'Fine. You sound worried. Is something bothering you?'

'No, I just happened to be thinking about her.' In fact, he had been thinking of the naked body of the girl in the ditch. 'Look after yourself.'

'And you . . .'

Chapter Eleven

Cynthia Bottrell sat at table eating toast thinly spread with low-fat margarine. Opposite her, across the table, her brother-in-law, James, decapitated a boiled egg. They were alone. The morning sun flooded the breakfast-room, merciless to already faded wallpaper and fabrics, searching out dusty ledges and cobwebbed corners. James reached for a slice of toast, broke off a piece and dipped it into his egg.

Cynthia said: 'You'll get salmonella poisoning, eating runny eggs.'

'I'm neither pregnant nor aged; in any case doctors have a professional immunity.'

The black marble clock on the mantelpiece had stopped but a little battery clock beside it showed fifteen minutes past eight.

Cynthia said: 'Are they going to arrest Lander?'

'I suppose so. I can't see what else they can do. They'll be searching his studio today for corroborative evidence. Poor old Simon is really up shit creek.'

'Don't be vulgar, James! I don't like it.'

'No, of course! I tend to forget you're not the woman I sometimes go to bed with in the afternoons. Interesting woman she is. You should meet her. At certain times her vocabulary seems to consist almost exclusively of four-letter words.'

Lady Bottrell flushed. 'You are a mean beast, James! Anyway, do you think Lander killed her?'

James looked up from his egg. 'How should I know?'

'I asked what you thought.'

'Then I think he did.'

Cynthia poured coffee and added a dash of milk. 'What about Tony Miller?'

For a while James went on eating as though he had not heard then, abruptly, he looked up: 'You know Miller came to see me on the night he was killed?'

'You told me; what about it?'

James was in no hurry; he reached for a fresh piece of toast and buttered it. 'We were talking about Lizzie Biddick and he said he didn't believe she'd gone to London or anywhere else. I asked him what he knew and he said he wasn't prepared to come out in the open with an accusation but that he'd dropped a strong hint in the right quarter.'

Cynthia was watching him, her cup half-way to her lips. 'The photograph sent to the police?'

'I suppose so. What else? He must have sent it, it would be too much of a coincidence otherwise.'

'And he got shot with his own gun. Have you said anything about this to Wycliffe?'

'No. I should be in trouble for not speaking sooner. In any case, he's got there without my help.'

Cynthia, whose hearing was acute, said: 'That's Hugh.' And she added in a low voice: 'This afternoon?'

'That's up to you. You know where I live.'

'Pig!'

Lord Bottrell came in, looking harassed. 'Where's Paul?'

'He went out early and he's not back yet.'

Bottrell, at the serving trolley, tipped muesli into a bowl and added milk. 'I'm worried about Lander; the police seem to have made up their minds and it can't be right. I don't believe it!'

Lady Bottrell said: 'You always were a trusting soul, Hugh.'

Kersey said: 'It's a classic case: eminently respectable professional man, middle-aged, repressed – no sexual experience to speak of and not much in prospect – suddenly finds himself with an attractive young girl on offer. He goes overboard, gets himself into a mess, is faced with blackmail – only one way out.'

He was breakfasting with Wycliffe in the alcove. A few empty tables separated them from the young couple whose attention was divided between the two policemen and the television news which had just carried an account of the finding of Lizzie Biddick's body.

'The naked body of a young woman, discovered yesterday by police searchers on the Duloe Estate in Cornwall, has been identified as that of Elizabeth "Lizzie" Biddick, absent from her home for several days. The dead girl, who was employed by Lord and Lady Bottrell, had recently announced her intention of going to work in London.

'Detective Chief Superintendent Wycliffe said last night that the death was being treated as a case of murder, the second on the estate in a few days. In the small hours of Monday morning Anthony Miller, the estate foreman, was shot dead in his cottage. The police are searching for a possible connection between the two crimes.'

The item was accompanied by stills showing the frontage of Duloe House, a view of King Harry ferry, and a long shot which could have been of the little promontory where the girl was found.

Wycliffe finished his bacon and reached for the marmalade. He said: 'You must listen to the tape. Lander's statement is oddly naive – especially coming from a lawyer. Once he was launched he sounded more like a boy of fifteen talking about his first girl, the nearest thing to calf-love I've come across in a long time.'

Kersey poured himself a second cup of coffee. 'He's boxing clever. With Fox about to turn over his nest there wouldn't be much point in denying anything so he turns on the Mills and Boon. All roses and stardust until some nasty man drops out of a tree, throttles the girl, and dumps her body and baggage on his doorstep.'

'And Miller?'

'Oh, Miller comes back from his holiday, starts asking awkward questions and poking around – getting dangerous.'

Wycliffe bit into his toast. 'And, of course, it was Miller who sent us the photographic tip-off just before getting himself shot. Doug! You have a Lewis Carroll talent for making nonsense sound like logic. And I suppose Lander is "the type"?'

Kersey believed – or said he did – in the theory of criminal types. Now he grinned. 'Of course! All sexually repressed lawyers over forty-five should be locked up as a preventive measure.'

Wycliffe walked slowly down the path towards Lander's studio. He could not have explained even to himself why he was on his way there. Fox would miss nothing and it would all appear in his report, but Wycliffe felt the need to renew his sense of place; he could not visualize a sequence of events out of their physical context.

It was half-past ten and the tide was an hour into the ebb. The mud was no more than a fringe between the water's edge and the rocky shale of the beach. A flotilla of swans cruised close inshore. Across the creek, the only other living creature in sight, a man, performed one of those arcane rites peculiar to the brotherhood of the boat:

standing in the stern of his craft he appeared to explore the bottom of the creek with a long pole.

Lizzie Biddick, then Tony Miller. Two murders which must be fitted into a pattern of interactive behaviour that was credible for the people concerned. 'Credible for the people concerned.' He spoke the words aloud.

Perhaps Lizzie had kept her appointment with Lander on that Sunday night: 'I was going to try to persuade her to stay – not to go away.' And if that persuasion had failed? Perhaps frustration and lust had erupted into an act of passion which is a euphemism for a sex killing. And the girl's body had been found naked in the ditch.

But she had been coshed before being throttled.

He arrived at the promontory where Lizzie's body had been found. The exact position, shielded from distant view by the scrub, was marked by pegs driven into the banks of the ditch. Otherwise there was nothing to tell of the drama which had so recently occurred. The gorse was bursting out in a late flowering and its scent lingered, while the bees made the most of it. Had Lander carried or dragged the girl's body from the house to the ditch? Fox had found no trace but that was not surprising having in mind the condition of the ground. It would be much more significant if, in the house, he found nothing to suggest that a crime had been committed there.

The house itself looked different, it no longer had that blind and deserted look; not only were the shutters open, but the windows too.

His presence had been observed. Fox met him at the door. With no preamble he launched into an account of his doings. 'I've finished upstairs, sir, and I'm now working in the studio itself.' With Fox it was always 'I', his assistant was rarely mentioned.

'Where is . . . ?' Wycliffe had to think what the young man was called. 'Where is Collis?'

'In the back yard. He's looking at an old shed where they used to keep coal and part of it was an earth privy.'

They were in the darkroom, no longer dark now that the shutters had been thrown back, and looking less mysterious though more tatty in the light of day.

'Anything upstairs?'

Fox looked aggrieved. 'A waste of time, sir. His prints and hers; a dressing gown and some casual clothes of his in the wardrobe, and that's it. He had a go at cleaning off prints but he wasn't very good at it. The bed sheets have been used but there's nothing to suggest any violence.'

Wycliffe said: 'You carry on. I'll take a look around.'

He climbed the narrow stairs. From a tiny landing at the top three rooms opened off: in one, a shower cabinet and WC; another was empty, and the third was the bedroom. If he had expected anything resembling a love nest he was disappointed; the furnishing was basic: a four-foot bed with a couple of pillows and a duvet; a wardrobe, a table, and an armchair. The whole lot could have been picked up in a saleroom at a knock-down price, and a bedroom in a back-street hotel could hardly have offered a less stimulating setting for illicit or any other kind of love.

There was a table beside the bed and, along with the alarm clock, there were copies of a highly technical photographic magazine.

What had the girl wanted from these men – from Lander, from James Bottrell, and from Tony Miller? And what had she got, apart from modest sums of money from Lander?

Wycliffe's thoughts drifted, vague and inconsequential, though underneath he was aware of a growing dissatisfaction with what he called Kersey logic: A kills B, C finds out, so A kills C. Put like that it sounded reasonable, but less so when one began to know the people involved and tried to link them with the details of what they were supposed to have done.

He was staring out of the bedroom window, at the creek, the swans, the boats, and the houses opposite. Suddenly it was as though time had been suspended and he experienced one of those moments which he had known since childhood when he looked about him and found everything strange and unfamiliar as though he had just arrived from some other place.

His mother had used to say: 'Why aren't you playing, Charles?' His teachers: 'Day dreaming again, Wycliffe!' From Helen it was: 'Penny for them.' Oddly, in his adult life at least, such experiences had seemed to anticipate some critical decision, or a decisive phase in whatever case he happened to be engaged. At least he went downstairs feeling, quite irrationally, that something had been achieved.

Fox was going through the metal drawers where Lander kept his collection of photographs. Of necessity it was a cursory examination as the drawers must have contained many hundreds, if not thousands.

Fox slipped easily into his lecture mode: 'Each photograph has its own envelope with details recorded on it and a catalogue number. The catalogue is cross-indexed so that any print can be traced under the name of the photographer, the year it was made, or the nature of the subject. Subjects are classified into—'

Wycliffe cut him short: 'But do they tell us anything relevant to the case?'

Fox removed his half-glasses and polished them. 'Perhaps not directly, sir, except that the envelope which contained the Nadar print is still there – empty. So it definitely came from here—'

'Anything else?'

'I believe the dead girl told her brother that Lander collected what she called "dirty pictures".'

'Well?'

Fox spread out a score or more postcard-size photographs which had been removed from their envelopes; they were mainly sepia prints, some of them slightly faded. 'Catalogued as "Parisian Brothel Scenes, 1880–1920", sir.'

Obviously the notorious 'French Postcards' produced for the tourist trade and covertly circulated well into the forties. Wycliffe supposed they were as much a part of the history of photography, at least of its social role, as most of the other specimens contained in the metal drawers.

Collis, Fox's assistant, arrived and stood, diffident, in the doorway.

Wycliffe was firmly convinced that dogs and their owners grow to look alike and was beginning to wonder if the same applied to scenes-of-crime officers and their assistants. Collis, who had started as a quite ordinary youth, seemed to grow daily more lean and lanky, his nose was becoming beaked, and he had the permanent air of an entomologist examining a specimen, or of a bird wondering whether a certain grub was good to eat.

'What is it, Collis?' Fox, abrasive.

Collis said: 'I think I've found her clothes.'

Wycliffe took over. 'Show me.'

In the yard, which was cut back into the hillside, there was a shed divided into two unequal parts; the larger part had been a fuel store; the smaller, an earth closet. The closet retained its bench-like seat with a hole in the top. What was not immediately obvious was that the seat was removable. Collis lifted it off, and in the cavity, on a floor of black soil, there was a small heap of clothing.

Fox said: 'Bags, Collis!'

Collis went out and returned with a pack of tagged polythene bags. Each item was placed in a separate bag: the orange blouse, the dark-blue trousers, the bra and briefs but no footwear. At the bottom of the little heap they found a plastic handbag.

As the items were being bagged it was obvious that dried leaves and even tiny twigs had become caught up in the folds or hitched in the weave of the materials. No botanist was needed to tell them that this detritus had been picked up in the neighbourhood of the ditch where the body was found. In other words, it was out there that the girl had undressed, or been stripped.

Fox said: 'Not very good at covering his tracks, was he?'

When Wycliffe returned to the Incident Van, Potter, the duty officer, was surreptitiously brushing crumbs from his shirt front like a schoolboy caught eating in class. Potter's paunch was of concern to Wycliffe and the hierarchy because it raised a question about his fitness for the job and had twice blocked his promotion.

'Not again, Potter!'

'I'm going without lunch today, sir.'

'Anything for me?'

'Dr Franks would like you to ring him before lunch, and Lady Bottrell has been, asking if you would call on her at your convenience. She was here about twenty minutes ago.'

'She was alone?'

'Yes, sir.'

'Agitated?'

Potter considered. 'More broody, I'd say.'

Wycliffe telephoned Franks, who said: 'I've completed the PM – nothing to report except that she was four months pregnant. I'm in a bit of a rush but I thought you would like to know.'

Something to think about. He dropped the telephone and turned to Potter: 'I shall be at the house.'

As he climbed the broad granite steps to the terrace he was suddenly a boy again, with his father and mother, all in their best clothes, attending the annual dinner provided by 'The Colonel' for his tenants. The Colonel would be standing at the top of the steps to greet his guests: 'Ah, Wycliffe! I hear you got yourself a couple of good heifers in last week's market . . . Mrs Wycliffe, always a pleasure . . . And this is young Charles . . .'

To the boy, Wycliffe, it had seemed that the family in the big house must lead very special lives, far removed from the rough and tumble of ordinary mortals. Even now he experienced a sense of let-down whenever he discovered that they, like the rest, may have their feet of clay.

His wife sometimes accused him: 'At heart, you're a snob, Charles!'

The door stood open to the bare hall; he pulled at the lever-like handle which operated the bell and heard it jangle in some remoteness. A moment or two later Lady Bottrell came to greet him.

'So good of you to come.' She lowered her voice. 'Hugh has had to take old Mr Lander into Truro. When he discovered that Simon was wanted here, nothing would satisfy him but that he should go to the office himself.'

Wycliffe was taken to the room overlooking the courtyard and they were about to sit down when her ladyship caught sight of Harry Biddick weeding the borders. 'On second thoughts we might be better in the library.'

The library was high, long, and narrow; bookcases reached half-way up the walls though their shelves were largely empty. Above the bookcases family portraits in massive gilt frames hid their faces behind layers of varnish and the accumulated dirt of years. A large Gothic window, with heraldic panels of stained glass, took up most of the end wall.

Wycliffe and her ladyship sat opposite each other at a huge oak table on which documents and leather-bound books were arranged in orderly heaps.

'Hugh spends his spare time sorting this stuff. Some of it, he thinks, could be valuable to historians.'

Lady Bottrell was, for once, off balance and talking too much. Her smooth forehead wrinkled: 'This is rather difficult. I find it hard to cope with the fact that you, until a few days ago a total stranger, are now acquainted with the more intimate details of our lives.' She looked at him with a tentative smile: 'I am not complaining; perhaps in a way it helps . . .'

Wycliffe, wearing what Helen called his 'cow look', said nothing.

Uncharacteristically restive as well as talkative, Cynthia fiddled with the pink tape which secured a sheaf of documents. 'I assume that what you have seen and heard this morning satisfies you that Lander was responsible for the terrible things that have happened here in the past fortnight.' Her blue eyes sought his – not, as novelists say, in mute appeal, but searchingly inquisitive.

His response was chilly: 'You have something to tell me, Lady Bottrell?'

Tacitly, she accepted that she was not going to be met halfway. 'I suppose I have. James has confided in me something which he should have told you at the start.'

Wycliffe waited.

'On the night he was murdered Tony Miller called on James and, in the course of conversation, he said that he was sure that Lizzie Biddick had not gone to London or anywhere else. Tony implied that he knew what had happened to her and who was responsible. He did not want to come out into the open with what he knew but he said that he had dropped a broad hint in the right quarter.'

When Wycliffe still remained silent she went on: 'It seems obvious that he was referring to the old photograph which he must have sent to you knowing that you would trace it to Lander's collection.'

'When did Dr Bottrell tell you this?'

'This morning, at breakfast.'

'Did he suggest that you should pass it on to me?'

'On the contrary, he said that you were getting there without his help.'

She was looking away from him, staring at the great window, patterned with its coats of arms. The sunlight, passing through the stained glass, made patches of colour on the dusty surfaces of the table and books.

'But you thought it right to tell me.'

She turned to face him with resolute candour. 'I wanted you to feel quite sure – not to have any doubts.'

It must have been obvious to her that something more was needed and she went on: 'I don't think you understand, Mr Wycliffe, all that lies behind the relationship between my husband's family and the Landers.' Again the faint smile. 'The Bottrell emblem is apt; they are very like cats; they appear to see nothing; in fact, they miss very little. But also like cats, they rarely trouble themselves to do much about what they see – or hear. James's attitude to what he heard from Tony Miller is typical.'

'Are you suggesting that Lander has taken unfair advantage of the family?'

An ironic laugh. 'That is an understatement, Mr Wycliffe! I am not, myself, in a position to point to anything specifically illegal but I know that the brothers could have made trouble for Lander over the administration of the estate and, in particular, over the handling of the late Lady Bottrell's personal affairs. She had substantial private means and both brothers were beneficiaries under her will.'

'Why, then, did they do nothing?'

Her reply was instant and she was flushed with indignation. 'Partly because they both share in the Bottrell malaise and, in any case, Hugh is blindly loyal to his friends – an expensive attribute where the Landers are concerned.'

Perhaps she had spoken with more warmth than she had intended, at any rate she felt the need to elaborate. 'They are greedy people, Mr Wycliffe, and Simon is an unpleasant person in other ways. James, for one, has good cause to know that.'

Wycliffe was watching her, dreamy-eyed, wondering how far he was being indoctrinated. He said: 'Having gone so far, Lady Bottrell, I think you must go a little further.'

She seemed to be studying the pattern of coloured lights which had just reached her hand as it rested on the table. 'It happened a long time ago, when they were children. The three boys: Hugh, James, and Simon were up in a tree-house they had in South Wood. Simon was an ungainly boy and it seems James made some derogatory remark about him, as boys will. Simon then, quite deliberately, reached out with his foot and pushed James off the little platform on which he was sitting.'

'He was injured?'

'A fractured tibia and a dislocated knee-joint. Of course it could not be proved, but it was thought that the injury to the knee was responsible for the subsequent tubercular condition which threatened his life and ruined his youth.'

'I suppose this created ill-feeling between the two families?'

Lady Bottrell made a helpless little gesture. 'Not in the least. If it had been Hugh the story would have been different, but the then Lady Bottrell had no use for her second son and the whole incident was treated as just one of the hazards of childhood.'

'And what was – what *is* James's attitude?'

She spread her hands. 'I don't know; I have never heard him refer to it. All I know I have learned from Hugh.'

A clock somewhere in the house chimed the three-quarters, a quarter to one. Wycliffe stood up and uttered the time honoured formula: 'Thank you for giving me your time, Lady Bottrell.'

'I hope that I haven't been indiscreet.'

Wycliffe felt sure that any indiscretion had been carefully calculated.

Chapter Twelve

'This case begins to look more like a detective story.'

Kersey was spooning clotted cream over his apple strudel. 'I wouldn't know, I never read 'em.'

Wycliffe said: 'You never read anything but the crime sheets, Doug.'

They were at lunch; the dining area was crowded and there was a buzz of conversation so that, for once, they felt reasonably secure in anonymity.

Lucy Lane said: 'In what way like a detective story?'

'It's over-complicated. The story writer creates a theoretical framework for a crime and by devising alibis and false trails he turns it into a test of wits. The real-life criminal, if he's going to get away with it, keeps it simple and, if we catch him, it's as much by luck as by cunning.'

Kersey, preoccupied, said: 'No more cream, Lucy? You won't taste that!' And turning to Wycliffe: 'Is there a moral in this, sir?'

Wycliffe, who had picked up his spoon, put it down again. 'Just that we seem to be dealing with artificially contrived situations, lacking spontaneity. The approach is theoretical; one has the impression that it's all in some script.'

It was unusual for Wycliffe to do his thinking aloud and he had captured Kersey's attention.

'I'm not sure that I follow.'

Wycliffe poured himself more wine and drank a little.

'It's as though the criminal, like an author contriving his plot, set out to decide how somebody would behave in a series of hypothetical situations. Having decided, he tried to make it appear that this person did, in fact, behave in that way.'

'You are saying that much of the evidence we have could have been rigged.'

'Most of it, I think.'

'With the deliberate intention of involving somebody else.'

'Yes. I was finally convinced by the finding of the girl's clothing in Lander's earth closet. But it began – for us – with Miller's rigged suicide; the short string, intended to draw attention to the phoney nature of the suicide, perhaps to hint that the killer was liable to panic.'

Lucy Lane, frowning, asked: 'In your opinion then, is there anyting in the way of direct evidence?'

Wycliffe was thoughtful. 'Yes, I think there is – the fact that Lizzie was coshed. That was something the killer was forced to do as a matter of expediency. He foresaw the necessity and provided for it, but I'm quite sure that he recognized it as a flaw in his plot. In my view, that is where we make contact with the killer instead of with his Frankenstein.'

'Does this let Lander off the hook?' From Kersey.

Wycliffe had not touched his sweet, now he pushed it aside. 'I've had growing doubts as to whether Lander would have been fool enough to incriminate himself in the wholesale fashion he seems to have done – panic or no panic. Of course it's possible that he's working a double bluff. We shall see.'

Wycliffe returned to the Incident Van shadowed, despite the appeal to the media, by a detachment of journalists.

For once he was able to satisfy them with a blend of fact and platitude so that they were soon on their way back to the pub.

It was hot, and although the windows of the van were open the air inside seemed turgid and sticky. To add to his discomfort his lunch, whatever it had been, lay heavily on his stomach and, whenever he looked out of the window, he was confronted by a Bottrell cat.

It was all very well fantasizing about creative criminals but the only evidence which counted in the courts was of the sort which would have satisfied St Thomas: it must be capable of being seen and touched or, at least, photographed.

Above all he needed to keep in the forefront of his mind that the girl was the primary victim. If the case was to make any sense at all, Miller's death followed from that. So the question was: why had Lizzie Biddick been murdered? And it had seemed reasonable to assume that she had raised unruly passions in the breast of a repressed, middle-aged lawyer.

According to the housekeeper Lizzie had left her room at about nine-thirty, presumably to say goodbye to James Bottrell and to keep her regular Sunday date at the studio. But that would be a special visit – her last. She was leaving for London in the morning. The encounter, *if* it took place, must have been highly emotional – at least for Lander, and it was not impossible that frustration and passion had got the better of him and that he had attacked and killed the girl.

A credible scenario – until one tried to fill in the detail. In the first place it was odd that the girl should have been coshed before being throttled, but setting that aside – along with the nature of the cosh itself, where would such a crime have taken place? Surely in the house. But Fox, an experienced scene-of-crime officer, had found no trace of any struggle – a fact which, though not conclusive, was highly suggestive.

Lizzie's body had been found naked in a ditch at some distance from the house and it would have made sense to carry it there in the hope of delaying discovery. But her clothing (except her shoes), bearing unmistakable signs of having been removed in the neighbourhood of the ditch, was found in a disused earth closet behind the house.

Wycliffe jabbed his ball-point into the scrap pad and pushed them both away. If Lander had killed the girl and disposed of her clothes, he must then have gone to her room, collected her more obvious baggage, and brought it back to hide in his well.

Rational behaviour? True, that killers are by no means always rational. Even so . . .

Wycliffe went in search of the Ninth Baron and found him in the main courtyard behind the house, washing his car. When he caught sight of Wycliffe he turned off the hose and wound it back on the reel.

There would be early photographs in the family albums showing the coach house and stables as they had been, with grooms and stable boys, perhaps an early motor car, sedate and strange on the cobbles, being polished by a chauffeur in striped apron, waistcoat, knickerbockers and leggings. Wycliffe wondered how it must feel to be the central character in a slow and tedious drama of decline.

'You wanted me?' Resigned.

'If you will spare me a few minutes, sir.'

Bottrell looked pale and weary, his eyes dark, as though he had lost sleep. 'My office? Or in the house?' He glanced at his watch. 'Better be the office.'

His secretary was tapping at her pre-war machine.

'Don't put through any calls, Delia.'

When they were seated Wycliffe said: 'I suppose you remember very clearly the incident in the tree?'

A quick look of surprise. 'The tree?'

'When your twin brother was injured.'

Bottrell studied his fingers. 'So that's it! My wife has been talking.'

Wycliffe said: 'In a murder case one looks for sources of enmity.'

'A quarrel between children forty-odd years ago – do you see that as a source of enmity today? I'm afraid I don't follow your line of thought.' His lordship being haughty.

'All the same, I shall be grateful if you will tell me what you remember of the tree-house incident.'

Bottrell hesitated, but decided on co-operation as the only practicable option. He opened the bottom drawer of his desk and brought out a stack of the sort of things people keep in bottom drawers. From it he sorted out a mounted photograph which he handed to Wycliffe.

The photograph was faded and looked as though it had once been framed. In fact there was a row of framed photographs above the bookcase and this might, at one time, have been one of them.

It showed three young boys in shorts, sitting on a platform built round a sturdy-looking tree-house. One of the boys wore a horn on a cord slung about his bare shoulders, the others had bows, and each had a wooden dagger at his waistband.

They were only eight or nine years old but there was no difficulty in identifying the young Lander. He was very thin, hollow-chested, and big-boned, but even then it was his thin lips and wide gape which gave him away.

Bottrell said: 'That was in the days when little boys pretended violence instead of watching it on the box.'

'You're the one with the horn?'

'Yes.'

'Is that where it happened?'

'Yes, in the same summer that was taken. James was sitting with his legs dangling over the edge as he is in the picture. Simon was behind him. James made some jibe at him about bed-wetting – he was always good at jabbing in the needle and, next minute, he was over the edge.'

'Pushed over.'

'I suppose so.' Bottrell became irritated. 'It's all so damned silly! If James hadn't been unlucky enough to injure himself nobody would have thought another thing about it. The drop was only a few feet.'

'But his injuries are supposed to have caused the tubercular lesion which resulted in his lameness.'

Bottrell pouted. 'That has been said, but I gather that independent medical opinion wouldn't necessarily agree.'

'However, since that incident, there has been ill-will between them?'

'I suppose that is true, James and Lander have never been on good terms, but I really cannot see the relevance of this to the . . . to the tragedies which you are investigating.'

His lordship had become flushed. 'Tony and the girl – what possible connection could their brutal murders have with a childhood quarrel between James and Lander?'

'That, sir, is what I am trying to find out, but I won't take up any more of your time.'

Bottrell followed him through the secretary's office to the outer door. 'I hope you won't think that I am being obstructive . . .'

'Not at all, Lord Bottrell. If it becomes necessary to return to the subject I will make sure that you have a reasoned explanation of my interest.'

Bottrell stood watching him as he crossed the courtyard to the arched entrance.

* * *

They were in the Incident Van; Kersey was smoking one of his home-mades, the windows were wide open but Lucy's whole being seemed to be concentrated in mute protest.

Wycliffe's thoughts were elsewhere. He turned to Lucy Lane first: 'I want you to pass instructions to Fox at the studio. He is to discontinue work there, put things back as nearly as possible as he found them and bring the key to me.'

'You mean, after he's finished?'

'I mean now.'

Kersey said: 'So you've made up your mind.'

Wycliffe ignored the remark and went on: 'I want you, Doug, to arrange for a round-the-clock watch on Lander – discreet. Choose men who know how to keep their heads down.'

'Is he free to come and go where and when he likes?'

'That is what I shall tell him directly.'

'Is he to be followed if he leaves the estate?'

'No; I'm only interested in his movements on the estate. Any contacts he makes while under observation are to be reported at once.'

Kersey's rubbery features creased in a grin. 'I think I've got the message.'

Jean answered his ring. The girl looked at him with expressionless eyes and did not speak.

'Is there somewhere we can talk?'

Without a word she pushed open the door of the drawing-room. In a cold, distant voice she said: 'Will you sit down?'

'No, this won't take long. I want you to cast your mind back to that Sunday, nearly a fortnight ago, when you and Paul went out at night together for the first time.'

She looked at him, and waited.

'Will you tell me what you did that night?'

'The same as last Sunday, we went out in the skiff.'

'Where did you go?'

'The Upper Creek, but because the tide was high we were able to go farther up; that first night we nearly reached the village.'

'So you passed your father's studio both going and coming, knowing that he was there, and you did more or less the same thing the following week?'

'Yes.'

'You were spying on him.'

She flushed. 'Not spying on him . . . It's just that he'd made the cottage into a sort of mystery place and—'

'All right; we won't play with words, Jean. Now, when you were out there last Sunday you saw a light in an upper room; did you see anything that earlier time?'

Her expression became wooden and she said nothing.

'You think I am trying to trap you but I can promise that what you tell me is unlikely to harm your father and might help him.'

She still hesitated but, in the end, in a dull monotone, she said: 'There was a light in the downstairs room when we went up.'

'And when you came back?'

'I hope you were telling the truth when you said it couldn't harm him.'

It was not what he had said but he let it pass. 'Well?'

'When we came back father was standing in the doorway of the cottage and he seemed to be staring out across the creek.'

'He didn't see you?'

'Because of the light from the doorway we saw him before he could see us. I told Paul to stop rowing and we waited until he went in.'

'How long?'

'About ten minutes.'

'Have you any idea of the time when this happened?'

'It was a quarter past one.'

'How do you know?'

'I happened to look at my watch while we were waiting.'

'Good!' And he meant it. The housekeeper claimed to have heard someone in Lizzie's room at five past one. It was a slender thread but it was enough. He said: 'I think you have helped your father. Now, perhaps you will tell him that I would like to see him.'

A moment or two later Lander came into the room. Wycliffe was shocked to see the change in him in so short a time; he seemed to have shrunk – a cliché, but somehow descriptive of a certain aspect of the effect of shock and despair. He was unshaven and his face was grey.

No greeting, he simply said: 'Do you want me to come with you?'

'No, I would like a talk.'

A look of mild surprise. 'I expected you, or somebody, earlier. I suppose this is all part of the technique. Anyhow you'd better come to my room.'

He led the way to a room at the end of a long passage. It was dominated by a Victorian bookcase and a massive table with an inset leather top. The table was littered with little heaps of pocket files secured by tape.

Lander pointed to an upright armchair and sat himself at the table where his spectacles rested on an open file. He sat motionless, waiting, as though he had surrendered all initiative.

Wycliffe took a key from his pocket and handed it across the table. 'We have finished at the studio. I hope that there has been no unnecessary disturbance. You are free to return there whenever you wish.'

Lander held the key in the palm of his hand for a moment, staring at it, then slipped it into his pocket.

Wycliffe waited for him to speak, but he did not. After a pause, Wycliffe said: 'As things are I think there is nothing to be gained from further questions or from interference with your movements or your property.'

Lander was turning over the papers in his file, apparently unaware of what he was doing. 'So you've decided that I didn't . . .' He paused, and seemed to choke over his words, 'that I didn't kill her.'

'As I interpret the evidence there is no case against you. I'm sorry that you have been subjected to all the strain and inconvenience but you brought it on yourself.'

Lander shook his head in a helpless gesture. 'What does it matter? . . . She's gone; Miller killed her. He was a pervert. Then he killed himself . . . There's no point in talking.'

Wycliffe said: 'Doesn't it seem to you strange that such an effort was made to incriminate you?'

'No, it does not. Miller knew that I was doing my utmost to get him off the estate.'

'Why the antagonism?'

A flash of anger. 'Because, as I've said, he was a pervert and he had corrupted Lord Bottrell.'

'That was how you saw it.'

'That is how it was!' There was a pause before Lander asked in a curiously humble voice: 'You will be leaving me alone now?'

It was a plain question, asked without obvious rancour, and Wycliffe, though doubtful of what was implied, said: 'Yes.'

He stood up, but the lawyer did not move. 'I'll see myself out.'

As he left the house Wycliffe asked himself why he had not mentioned Lizzie's pregnancy and the only answer he could find disturbed him, because it was unprofessional.

Chapter Thirteen

When Wycliffe awoke he was aware of a change; the light was grey, no sunlight filtered through the flowered curtains, and the air felt different – still warm, but humid. When he parted the curtains it was to see the whole sky a canopy of cloud, leaden grey with a faintly coppery hue.

It was exactly a week since he and Helen had returned from the Dordogne.

Downstairs, at the alcove table, Kersey said: 'Weather's on the change.' If there had been a barometer Kersey would have tapped it. The young couple had switched on the television and the medicine man from the Met was expounding the threatening nature of his animated maps: 'Thunderstorms over France and the channel are expected to move northwards during the day and there will be outbreaks of heavy rain accompanied by thunder in much of south-west Britain . . .'

As usual, the landlord, in singlet and trousers, stood in the doorway smoking a cigarette, while the cat, on the step at his side, attended to her toilet. But the atmosphere had changed; now the stillness seemed charged and menacing. Wycliffe wondered if it was really the weather or his inner trepidation. He was worried. Satisfied that he had arrived at some understanding of the case, he knew that he had no evidence on which to proceed. He could wait for something more to happen and pray that it wouldn't be another tragedy. (He thought that he had taken reasonable precautions.) Or he could precipitate a crisis and risk finding himself in free fall without a parachute.

In company with Kersey he was at the Incident Van shortly after eight-thirty. The overnight surveillance report on Lander was unexciting. Just before dark the lawyer had left the house and made for his studio; there he had opened the shutters of the studio room. For an hour, he could be seen at his desk, writing; then he had pulled down the blind, but the light had remained on all night.

Wycliffe asked Dixon, the duty officer: 'Nothing since?'

'Nothing, sir.'

Almost as they spoke the radio came alive: '105 to Zero Oscar . . .' There was urgency in the voice.

'Go ahead.'

'I couldn't make contact; I must have been in a dead spot. Lander's got visitors. Within the past couple of minutes Lord Bottrell and his brother James arrived and went inside.'

Wycliffe reached for the head-set. 'Wycliffe here. Go in after them. Any pretext, but don't be put off. I'll be right down.' He turned to Dixon: 'Who is it down there?'

'PC Watts, sir, a young chap from the local nick. Supposed to be one of the new whizz kids – just passing through.'

'You come with me.' To Kersey.

The tide was at flood, the highest he had yet seen it; the creek was a broad silvery sheet under a lowering sky; almost every scrap of colour had disappeared from the landscape. As they reached the little building on the strand Wycliffe felt two large, warm raindrops on his forehead and thought he heard a grumbling of thunder in the distance.

The door was open and they found the Bottrell brothers in the darkroom. PC Watts, in a track suit, was standing in the doorway of the studio.

'Mr Lander is dead, sir. These two gentlemen found him. I asked them to stay in this room until you arrived.'

Lord Bottrell was about to speak but Wycliffe stopped him. 'Just one moment . . .'

Wycliffe and Kersey went through into the studio, followed by the young policeman. The shutters were folded back but the blind was no longer down although the electric light was still on.

Lander was lying on the floor as though he had slipped out of his chair; his body was rigid, and his head twisted to one side. There was foam about his lips and the jaws appeared to be tightly clenched; his eyes were open and staring. His skin, which had been strikingly pale, now had a pinkish hue. On the floor near the body were two or three gelatine capsules of the sort used for the oral administration of unpalatable drugs.

In a low voice Wycliffe spoke to Watts. 'Where were they when you joined them?'

'In here, sir. Dr Bottrell was on his knees by the body; I fancy he was sniffing at the dead man's lips.'

'Did they offer any explanation of how they came to be here?'

'Lord Bottrell said that Mrs Lander had telephoned him, worried that her husband hadn't come home to breakfast, and because she got no answer when she telephoned here. It seems she never comes near the studio herself.' Watts added: 'I gather the lady is inclined to over-react.'

Kersey snapped: 'Well it looks as though she had something to react about. This blind was still down when you relieved the night man; who raised it?'

'One of the brothers, sir, before I got here.'

'How long did they have in here before you eventually got round to joining them?' Kersey disliked young coppers who fancied their chances in the fast lane.

Watts was as curt as he dared. 'The time it took me to make radio contact and receive instructions. Probably a little over two minutes.'

Wycliffe said to Kersey: 'You'd better get hold of the local GP – Prentiss, isn't it?'

Watts volunteered: 'Dr Bottrell phoned him, sir. It seemed the right thing to do so I didn't interfere.'

'All right; ask Dr Bottrell to come in.'

Bottrell came in, loose and large, his Viyella shirt open down the front, his trousers sagging from the belt. 'Hugh and I were having breakfast when Beth Lander phoned. One of her panics. Hugh said he would look in at the studio so I walked down with him. I suppose your constable told you that I've telephoned Prentiss. He was out on his rounds but they're contacting him.'

Lord Bottrell appeared in the doorway, harassed and diffident: 'Mrs Lander will be expecting to hear from me . . . I think I should telephone my wife and ask her to break the news . . .'

Wycliffe said: 'There's no reason why you shouldn't do it in person, if you wish, Lord Bottrell. There will be time enough for your statement later.'

When his lordship had gone Wycliffe turned to the brother. 'Poison, is that how you see it?'

James shrugged. 'What else? Probably cyanide. I caught a whiff when I bent over him just now. You know he dabbled in archaic photographic techniques in that witches' kitchen next door. Didn't they use cyanide of potassium or sodium as a reducing agent or something? Anyway, Prentiss will be here directly, do you want me to stay?'

Wycliffe, anxious for room to manoeuvre, said: 'No, I

shall be asking you for a statement later and any professional observations you feel inclined to make can wait until then.'

Dr Bottrell limped away and Kersey watched him go as a cat watches an escaping bird. 'I don't like that bastard! I'm not suggesting that he killed Lander – suicide sticks out a mile – but there's something about that man . . .'

Wycliffe was gazing out of the window. Blue-black clouds lowered over the creek; the light was pale and limpid, but the little houses opposite stood out seeming strangely near. Raindrops trickled down the window panes as though the great sponge of cloud was being gently squeezed, but the threatened storm had not yet broken. In the studio the yellow light from the electric lamp struggled against the light of day.

The rain finally arrived as James Bottrell reached his own door. It was prefaced by a dramatic blue lightning flash, a searing sound as of material being ripped across, and a great thunderclap which echoed and rumbled through the shuddering air.

Instantly rain bounced off the cobbles forming spray which rose like a mist into the air; gutters were soon choked and water cascaded from the roofs so that within minutes the whole yard was awash. Another brilliant flash, a simultaneous thunder-clap, and the rain seemed to hesitate as the storm drew breath, only to resume seconds later with renewed ferocity.

Bottrell stood just inside his door, leaving it open. Anarchic nature suited his mood. He was excited, tense with anticipation. When he finally closed the door, the high, church-like room seemed to be in almost total darkness. Not troubling with the main lights, he crossed to the table and switched on a desk-lamp at the place where he usually worked. There, in the little island of light, before sitting down, he drew from his hip pocket an envelope, sealed, and inscribed: 'To Jean'. Sitting at the table, he slit it open and removed from it several sheets of thin paper which he unfolded and spread out to read.

The letter began: 'My dear Jean, I feel that it is to you that I owe an explanation of what has happened and of what I am about to do . . .'

The lawyer's handwriting, starting off bold and clear, degenerated almost to illegibility but James persevered to the end. It really was amusing, but what impressed him was the extent to which he seemed to be in the hands of a benevolent fate. By chance he had gone down with his brother in response to Beth Lander's appeal. By chance Hugh, with his usual timidity, had hung back, leaving him to investigate the premises alone and to find, not only Lander's body, but also this bizarre valediction. He had taken it thinking that Lander might have entertained some suspicion of him, or at least that his name would be mentioned . . .

He need not have troubled himself. He was being altogether too wary; he should trust in his karma.

He reached for a hard-covered manuscript book labelled in bold lettering on the front: *Case Book VI*.

There were similar books on a shelf among the box files but these were his notes on cases he had handled professionally. *Case Book VI* was special; it concerned himself. He opened the book; most of the pages were blank but the earlier ones were covered in his surprisingly small and neat script. He selected a passage and read with total absorption, as though from some fascinating work of another hand:

'I wish that I could put on record my precise state of mind at the moment when I decided to kill her, and recount the processes of thought which led me to that decision. I cannot. There was no such moment and, as far as I am aware, there was no decision. I only know that the deed became compelling and inevitable.

'I do recall with remarkable clarity and vividness that night, a week earlier, when she told me that she was pregnant, but I cannot say whether or not that incident played any part in determining the course of events. I doubt it; I doubt it very much.

'It was a banal occasion. "You know that I am pregnant by you and that I am going away. I think you should give me some money." No threats. Indeed, she could have done nothing beyond complicating my life for a little while. She stood there – a peasant girl, with a certain prettiness that was already a little over-ripe. There was a dogged look in her brown eyes; her obstinate little mouth was daubed with lipstick, and tight trousers accentuated her thick thighs . . . Flesh without mind.

'I found her repulsive and could not believe that I had ever sought pleasure in her body. However, I told her that when she was settled in London I would regularly pay money into her account and, with this, she was not only satisfied, but cloying in her gratitude.

'As I have said, I do not think the incident changed anything. On the night before she was due to leave I waited for her at the creekside where she would pass on her way to Lander's studio . . .'

Bottrell raised his eyes from the book to dwell on the images which these words had conjured out of the past and it was through his unaided memory that he now followed in exquisite detail the further events of that night to their climax.

Dr Prentiss arrived shortly after the storm had broken, his blond hair darkened and flattened by rain. He placed his bag on Lander's desk and removed his waterproof which dripped to the floor. 'They caught me on my rounds.' The young man looked harassed, as well he might. 'Are you treating this as suicide?'

'Until we find evidence to the contrary.'

'But Dr Franks will be in on it?'

'In all the circumstances.'

Rain lashed against the window. At short intervals lightning forked over the creek in jagged streaks, followed instantly by the thunder-clap and great earth-shaking rumbles . . .

Prentiss stood for a while, staring down at the body, then he dropped to his knees and went through the limited routine permitted to him: sniffing, palpating the exposed flesh, and testing the flexure of the limbs. When he was once more on his feet, he said: 'Obviously a respiratory poison; I suppose it could be cyanide.' He stooped to examine the capsules on the floor then picked one up and held it in the palm of his hand.

The capsule was half red and half black with the word 'Penbritin' neatly printed in white lettters on the black half.

Wycliffe asked: 'Can you tell me anything about them?'

'Penbritin is a trade name for a synthetic penicillin used to treat Gram negative bacterial infections – anything from 'flu to meningitis.'

Kersey demanded: 'Prescribed by you?'

Kersey received a cold stare. Prentiss was finding his dignity. 'No, I have never treated Mr Lander although he is on my list. It's possible that he got them from my predecessor. I shall check the records.'

He turned back to Wycliffe but had to wait before he could make himself heard against the rain and the reverberations of thunder. Then: 'More to the point now, these capsules separate very easily into two halves and can be put together again.'

Wycliffe said: 'You are saying that substitution of the contents would be easy.'

'Very.'

Kersey tried again: 'So you think he was murdered.'

'Do I? Perhaps you will explain.' Acid.

'Why would he go through all that rigmarole to poison himself?'

'I can think of one reason: I'm told that cyanide is decidedly unpalatable as well as distressing in its effects, but Lander could have swallowed any number of these before the first began to release its contents in the stomach making him wish he'd thought of something else.'

Wycliffe was brooding. 'Assuming that it was cyanide I suppose death would follow quickly upon ingestion.'

Prentiss ran a hand through his wet hair. 'I'm no toxicologist. All I can say is that the active agent is hydrocyanic acid and the effectiveness of any of the cyanide salts depends on the rate at which the acid is released in the stomach.'

'But minutes rather than hours.'

Prentiss put on his waterproof and picked up his bag. 'Probably. Now, if that is all I'll get back on my rounds. I'll let you have my report.'

Wycliffe thanked him. When the doctor had gone, Kersey grinned. 'That young man is learning! He must also be keen, to go to his patients in this.'

At that moment a double fork over the creek was followed by the loudest crack yet; the light flickered but recovered.

When they could once more hear themselves speak Kersey said: 'Don't you think it's odd that Lander didn't leave a kiss-me-good-bye-note – even a confession?'

'Perhaps he posted it to the coroner.' Wycliffe was preoccupied, dismissive. 'But speaking of the coroner, it's time we notified him. Then get Fox down here – No, not Fox – get somebody from division; I shall want Fox. I've no doubt this is suicide but we have to have confirmation. So, formal statements from all concerned; these capsules must go for analysis; we need to know the source and exact nature of the poison . . . But delegate all this; I want you back at the van as soon as possible.'

Kersey was looking at him with a puzzled frown. 'Did you think that Lander might kill himself?'

'The short answer to that is, no. If I had . . .'

'Then you must have thought he was at risk from someone else, or that he was dangerous on the loose.'

Wycliffe was curt. 'I thought that he might be at risk, and I took precautions.'

Kersey persisted: 'Isn't the most likely explanation of his death that he killed himself because he was guilty, knew that we could get him, and couldn't face it?'

Wycliffe made an obvious effort: 'Think of it from his point of view, Doug; he's lost the only woman with whom he seemed able to establish an emotional relationship and he's faced with an inquest which is sure to bring out details of the affair for public gossip. He'd lost both ways. And that's ignoring complications within his family. For anybody, a daunting prospect, but for a small-town, middle-aged lawyer . . .'

Kersey said: 'You speak of an inquest, not about proceedings in the criminal court.'

'Lander believed that Miller killed the girl, so with Miller dead there could be no criminal charge.'

Kersey looked at Wycliffe with an odd expression in which serious doubt mingled with an indulgent affection: 'And how do you see it, sir? Is there going to be a criminal charge at the end of this lot?'

Wycliffe looked at him, a deeply worried man. 'My God, I hope so!'

For a long time James sat, staring into space and when he eventually moved he was like a man emerging from the deepest sleep. He looked about him, at first with a certain wonder, then with increasing awareness as though taking aboard the trappings of his daily life and resuming contact.

The storm centre had moved away, an occasional lightning flash dispelled the gloom and thunder rumbled in the distance, but the rain continued unabated, battering on the roof which, like the roof of a church, was open to the rafters. He was still seated, irresolute, when someone banged on the door and kept up a steady pounding. He closed his book, got up from his chair and walked to the door. Before opening it he took time to compose his features and to recover his customary manner and poise.

It was Jean Lander, soaked to the skin and deeply distressed.

She walked past him into the room without a word and went to stand by the table, her back towards him. Her shoulder-length red hair hung like rats' tails, T-shirt and jeans clung dripping to her body, her sandals oozed and squelched.

She said: 'I walked out on mother; I couldn't stand it. I mean, with what had happened to father she couldn't say a good word about him. You would think he did it just to . . . to inconvenience her!' She spat out the words.

He was still so tense that he could scarcely speak but he achieved a banal question: 'You walked out in this weather?'

'It wasn't raining then; I got caught in South Wood.' She added, her eyes wide: 'I can't go back – not yet!'

He was growing calmer and thinking fast. 'You'd better change into something so that we can dry your things. In the wardrobe, in that room at the top of the stairs, you'll find a woman's dressing gown – you can wear that. And the slippers might fit . . . There are towels in the cupboard under the washbasin. Is there anybody with your mother?'

'Uncle Hugh and Aunt Cynthia.'

He was pleased with himself; she seemed to have noticed nothing.

He watched her climb the spiral staircase, a dejected figure. He found a portable electric fire, plugged it in, and arranged a chair on which to hang her clothes.

A few minutes later she came down wearing Cynthia's blue dressing gown, and slippers. She had dried her hair and now her pale face was framed in a rufous halo. She carried her wet clothing which she gave him when he held out his hand. 'I tried to wring them out.'

He draped the chair with her jeans, her T-shirt and her briefs – all there was apart from her sandals which he placed near the fire.

'Thanks, James.' She sounded tired to the brink of exhaustion.

He noted with satisfaction that she called him by his first name, while Hugh and Cynthia were courtesy 'Uncle' and 'Aunt'.

'Get yourself warm; you mustn't catch a chill.' He placed another chair near the fire.

He was being solicitous and, as always when he did not understand the sources of his own behaviour, he was troubled. The girl did not interest him; even sexually he was not attracted; her occasional visits were no more than an entertaining diversion and, at the moment, she was intruding on his privacy.

Yet he could not take his eyes off her.

She sat, her red hair hanging free and covering her face; her legs were crossed at the knees under the skirt of the dressing gown, and she was bending over, massaging a bare foot.

It was as he continued to watch her that an idea came to him, an idea so intriguing yet so simple that he could scarcely contain his excitement.

He said, softly: 'Jean!'

She turned to face him.

'There is something I ought to give you. You know that it was I who found your father?'

'Yes.'

'On his desk there was a letter.'

'A letter? Uncle Hugh said that he had left nothing . . .'

'Hugh didn't see it; I was alone in the room. There was no envelope but I could see that it was for you and of such a personal nature that you wouldn't want the police or any stranger to read what he had written.'

She was incredulous. 'You mean he wrote to me?'

He crossed to the table and she followed him, he handed her the pages of her father's letter and she looked from them to him, uncertain.

'I should read it now; perhaps it will tell you something you want to know.'

He placed a chair for her but she remained standing, the letter in her hand.

His eyes never left her face as she read; he saw her expression change from incredulity to wonder, and from wonder to pain. He saw cheeks become flushed and tears form between her lashes.

Her neck was slender and long, and lightly freckled; she wore a silver filigree pendant set with a blue stone. He knew now why, and for what he had waited. This time he would not be staring into bland unconsciousness, he would watch the fleeting expression of those features and those eyes as astonishment was succeeded by fear and fear by terror; terror which would become petrified by death.

There would be tremendous risk. But had he not shown that he could cope with any situation? He had been too timid, and timidity now would cost him precious and unimagined sensations.

The moment would come when she finished reading the letter and turned to him for support, sympathy, or whatever else her tedious little mind found necessary to restore its equilibrium.

Chapter Fourteen

Wycliffe's departure from the cottage was undignified as well as uncomfortable. He climbed the now slippery path to Lander's drive wearing a plastic bag over his head but he was rescued at the top by a crime car, stationed there to pick him up. Back in his cubicle, he drank strong coffee, troubled by disturbing thoughts and a sense of guilt. He could not rid himself of the memory of Lander in that last interview or of the pathos in the lawyer's question: 'You will be leaving me alone now?'

Next door, Lucy Lane drank her coffee while vetting and filing reports. In reception, Potter, mortally scared of thunderstorms, let his grow cold, and he would have fingered a rabbit's foot, had he possessed one.

The roof of the van resounded to the rain like a drum and the whole area around the Duloe entrance was a sea of thin mud. Wycliffe telephoned sub-division and spoke to DI Reed – Tom Reed – who had been in at the start. Wycliffe brought him up to date against a background of thunder-claps and crackles on the line which threatened the connection.

'Now I want you to get me a search warrant, Tom. I'll send a DC along and he'll give you the specifics. He's to bring it back here and I'll leave word what's to be done with it.'

Wycliffe was worried, well aware that he was banking heavily on his reading of a man's mind – and on bluff. The thunderstorm was moving away but the rain continued unabated for a while, then stopped as abruptly as it had begun. He was waiting for Kersey, but decided to wait no longer. He called Lucy Lane and they set off together, leaving word for Kersey to follow.

They went in a crime car, with Lucy driving; they passed between the granite pillars with their newly bathed cats and along the drive. Leaves, twigs, and even small branches had been battered from the trees, a legacy of the storm, but there was also a freshness in the air, sharp and exhilarating. They made for the back of the house and passed under the stone arch into the main yard. The place was deserted. Great puddles, amounting to pools, covered much of the yard. Lucy negotiated the narrow, angled entrance to the stable yard and pulled up outside the varnished door.

As on another occasion the door was not quite closed but this time, without knocking, Wycliffe pushed it wide. The sight which met his eyes would always remain in his memory. In the gloom, two figures, a man and a young girl, stood close. The girl, her red hair swept back, wore a blue dressing gown and in one hand she held a little sheaf of crumpled papers. The man stood over her, his arms raised as though arrested in some action or gesture. The light from the high window fell full on their faces. Bottrell's expression was concentrated – intense; while Jean, her cheeks blotched and tear-stained, looked up at him in astonishment and dawning terror.

There was a stillness in the scene, as in a photograph, but there was also menace.

Wycliffe was half-way towards the couple when Bottrell turned his head to look at him, uncomprehending. The man was abnormally pale, his eyes were vacant, and there was an interval before blankness gave place to unease. He was the first to speak: 'Jean was caught in the storm and she came here.' He sounded hoarse.

The girl, still clutching her papers, seemed paralysed. Lucy Lane went to her and murmured something.

Wycliffe, too, was striving to re-orientate himself; he felt like an actor who, having mastered his part, finds himself in the wrong play. He felt strangely short of breath and his words, when they came, seemed absurdly inadequate: 'Does Mrs Lander know that Jean is here?'

There was a perceptible pause before Bottrell answered, 'No.'

But Wycliffe spoke to the girl with great gentleness: 'Jean, will you let Miss Lane take you home? There's a car outside and you can take your wet clothes with you.'

She looked at him as though she too were making a slow return from some other realm of consciousness, then she nodded.

Lucy collected the clothing and followed the girl out. The letter went with her but Wycliffe could leave that to Lucy.

Bottrell watched and listened, but said nothing.

Wycliffe turned to him. 'Sit down!' It was an order.

Without a word, Bottrell went to his usual chair where a desk-lamp made a pool of yellow light on the table. In front of him was a hard-covered manuscript book labelled: *Case Book VI*.

Wycliffe sat in the chair opposite, across the table.

Bottrell, still vague and uncoordinated, muttered: 'I need a drink.' He got up and went to a small cupboard below the shelves of box files; he fumbled for a moment or two then returned with a gin bottle and a glass. He poured himself three fingers, drank it off in a couple of gulps, then poured the same again.

For Wycliffe it was a much needed respite.

In a very short time colour had returned to Bottrell's cheeks, his facial muscles seemed to recover their tone, his eyes were once more focused. With an expansive gesture he said: 'Shall I get you a glass?'

Wycliffe shook his head and Bottrell held up the bottle: 'Holland's gin! All down to a seventeenth century medico at Leyden – concocted from juniper berries as a medicine!'

In his anxiety to appear normal he was overdoing the act. He drank a little more gin, wiped his lips, and put his glass down.

'So it's over! . . . Not a very satisfactory case from your point of view, I suppose. The good news is that Lander has saved you a hell of a lot of paper work.'

As he sought for and almost found his usual wavelength Bottrell settled more comfortably in his chair. 'Incidentally I have to admit to an indiscretion. Lander left a sentimental letter addressed to Jean, and I pocketed it . . . Decided to give it to the girl myself instead of having your minions make a meal of it . . . You came in the middle of her reading the thing and now it's gone with her . . . No harm done.'

Wycliffe sat still, his gaze expressionless.

Bottrell looked at him, expectant, perhaps troubled by his total lack of response. He paused, long enough to light a cigarette. 'You see, Wycliffe, Lander was emotionally retarded . . . He'd never discovered what it was all about and how to handle it at the proper age, and so we have this romantic schoolboy act from a man of fifty. As to Lizzie . . . Lizzie was fluttering around, picking up this and that – a magpie for experience. She wasn't particularly interested in sex but like most women she delighted in contriving situations which made her the centre of attention. But Lizzie had no notion of a settled relationship, legitimate or otherwise . . .'

Bottrell waved his cigarette in a dismissive gesture. 'Of course, to a normal man, Lizzie was no more than an amusing diversion, but to Lander she was a match to the blue touch-paper—'

With total irrelevance Wycliffe cut across this chatter, which he had scarcely heard, and crystallized the only thoughts in his mind: 'Jean Lander was within moments of her death! You would have killed her!' In his agonizing attempt to confront the monstrous possibility that he might have arrived too late he could only repeat the accusation: 'You would have killed her, you bastard!'

The afternoon was clear and cool; great billowy white clouds floated in a blue sky – English weather – a staple product before the Met people discovered computers and invented global warming. Once more Wycliffe made for the stable yard and the varnished door.

The interior was transformed by lights, pendant from the roof beams; they must have been there all along but were now switched on. The effect was demeaning, exposing a dusty shabbiness and chasing mystery away. Fox and Collis were there. An area of the big table had been cleared and on it was a collection of polythene bags, duly tagged. Wycliffe, feeling detached – remote – said: 'They are not our bags.'

'No, sir. This is just how I found the stuff, in a cupboard next to the one where he keeps his gin. You might say, they're exhibits from his private black museum. These things are all directly connected with the two killings.'

Wycliffe picked up the first of the bags to catch his eye: 'C.B. VI.1.E.B. Rubber truncheon (See also C.B.IV.14) now, with adherent hair.' Through the polythene, Wycliffe caught the gleam of a long, black hair adhering to the roughened surface of the rubber.

Fox said: 'The code refers to his case book and E.B. must be Elizabeth – Lizzie – Biddick, sir.'

'Thank you, Fox.'

A small bag, appropriately labelled, held Lizzie's pendant and chain; a large one, had its contents listed as: 'Miller's diary and selected letters.' A third, small but gruesome, held a handkerchief, heavily stained with what purported to be Miller's blood . . . Lizzie's sandals were in yet another bag – the missing items from her clothing found in the earth closet.

Fox, slipping for once into the vernacular, said: 'We've got a nutter, sir!'

Wycliffe picked up Bottrell's case book and turned the pages. It would prove a rich diet for the contending lawyers and their consultant psychologists and psychiatrists. Bottrell would be squabbled over by a flock of his professional peers and if ever the case came to court he would be the star of a drama in which Lizzie Biddick and Tony Miller – like Hamlet's father, would have only bit parts.

'Do you think we do a worthwhile job, Fox?'

'I try not to think about it, sir.'

'I look forward to the time when I shall have the leisure to analyse my motives in choosing Lander as the scapegoat.'

Bottrell sat back in his hard chair, blew a smoke ring and watched it rise. 'Of course he was the obvious choice – the man was making a fool of himself with the Biddick girl and if anything happened to her he was sure of top billing in the list of suspects.

'What you don't know is that I *contrived* that relationship – I put her up to it . . . Oddly enough, the stupid girl went soft on him but it was I who set it up. So, I ask myself, did I have it in my mind even then that I might one day kill her? You will see from my case book that I can't decide at what stage that act became inevitable.

Was it before or after she confronted me with the news of her pregnancy? Was it, perhaps, long before that – when I first met her?'

The scene was an interview room at sub-division where any fly on the wall was living through a unique experience; certainly neither Wycliffe nor the middle-aged copper standing by the door, had ever known anything like it. Almost from the moment of Wycliffe's dramatic accusation Bottrell had seemed to accept, even to anticipate his fate; now in the dreary little interview room it was as though he relished the prospect before him.

'You'll find more than enough to put me away.'

He had refused a solicitor and declined to answer questions, but volunteered to 'discuss his case'. This was officially interpreted as agreeing to make a statement and that statement was now being recorded on tape.

He leaned forward to engage Wycliffe's attention more closely: 'You see, Wycliffe, the apparently rational processes of the conscious mind are often no more than surface manifestations of turmoil, deep in the unconscious. I wonder sometimes whether Lander was my target from the first, and the girl only a means to an end.'

He was frowning, speaking with great earnestness. 'But if that is so, how far did it arise from that episode, forty-odd years ago, when Lander pushed me out of a tree for saying he peed in his sleep?'

Suddenly Bottrell's features and his whole body relaxed; he grinned broadly. 'Absurd, isn't it? But no more so than most of our efforts to masquerade as rational beings.'

Once more Wycliffe was a captive audience, listening to the narcissistic outpourings of a disordered mind.

'I got a kick out of fixing Lander – calculating the extent to which his essential stupidity would off-set his cunning if ever he decided to kill. And then I contrived the thing as it seemed to me he would have tackled it – with that fatal blend of bravado and panic. My problem was that he was no killer – he lacked the moral courage – he was hard, but brittle – no fibre. It was an unconscious recognition against his guilt.'

The window was high, but the sound of constant traffic on the roundabout outside, with the occasional squeal of brakes or screech of tyres, furnished a background for all that was said and done in the little room.

'Did you expect that Lander would kill himself?'

Bottrell blew out a cloud of grey smoke. 'It was on the cards but I didn't count on it.'

An hour later they were still there; a break had been called for refreshments and when they resumed, Bottrell took a cigarette from the pack on the table and lit it.

'This interview resumes at 12.28 hours.'

Bottrell said: 'Killing Miller was a simple necessity. He mentioned, quite casually, that the girl had told him she was pregnant by me. It meant nothing much to him then but it would have meant a great deal when her body was found and he realized that she had been murdered.

'It happened that I had borrowed his gun before he went on holiday so, on the Sunday night, I returned it, and rigged my little charade for your people – short string and all. It seemed to me the sort of stupidity which would have marred any attempt by Lander to lay a false trail.'

Bottrell tapped ash from his cigarette into the tin lid provided. For a moment or two his grey-green eyes were unfocused and he seemed lost in thought. It was quiet now, the traffic outside had dwindled to an occasional car as evening settled over the town.

'Then there was the photograph – the famous Nadar

print.' Bottrell smiled. 'Lizzie gave it me – she was always giving me things, trying to buy attention. It occurred to me that by amending it and sending it to you I could ensure that Lander was put squarely in the frame . . . And it worked, didn't it?'

Another silence, and Bottrell yawned, throwing back his arms. 'God, I'm tired! In any case I think I've said all I want to say except that you and I will be plagued by psychiatrists and psychologists. They will fight first over whether or not I am fit to stand trial and there will be some nice fat fees for the taking . . . I only hope that Meyrick – a former colleague – is in on the act; it would make it all worth while to lead the old windbag up the garden.'

Sunday morning; the church bells were ringing, the sky was clear blue but there was just a touch of autumn in the air. Now the investigation would wind down but, in offices far from the valley of the Fal, discussions would soon begin concerning a possible case: R. v Bottrell. A decision would have to be made – whether or not Bottrell was fit to plead. Those involved would know nothing of Duloe or Treave, and nothing of the people who lived and died there – except what they found in the files. As for Wycliffe, although his investigation was all but over, many months would go by before he heard the official last of the case.

He found Kersey in the Incident Van smoking a real cigarette and reading a transcript of the Bottrell interview. Kersey pushed the papers away, uncommonly subdued: 'It seems to me that we deal with two kinds of real criminal – the merely wicked, and the truly evil; those with some sense of guilt and those with none; they either have a conscience, or they don't.'

Wycliffe was standing, looking out of the window.

'Your terminology is old-fashioned, Doug; Bottrell diagnosed his own case as "arrested development of the super-ego as a consequence of parental indifference".'

Kersey said: 'I call that passing the buck.'

'So do I, but what of the sins of the fathers – and mothers?' Wycliffe was looking up at one of the gateposts for perhaps the last time. 'Anyway, I hope those bloody cats have nightmares!'

THE END

available from

THE ORION PUBLISHING GROUP

☐ Wycliffe and Death in Stanley Street £5.99
W.J. BURLEY
0-7528-4969-7

☐ Wycliffe and the Scapegoat £5.99
W.J. BURLEY
0-7528-4971-9

☐ Wycliffe in Paul's Court £5.99
W.J. BURLEY
0-7528-4932-8

☐ Wycliffe and the Quiet Virgin £5.99
W.J. BURLEY
0-7528-4933-6

☐ Wycliffe and the Tangled Web £5.99
W.J. BURLEY
0-7528-4446-6

☐ Wycliffe and the Cycle of Death £5.99
W.J. BURLEY
0-7528-4445-8

☐ Wycliffe and the Last Rites £5.99
W.J. BURLEY
0-7528-4931-X

☐ Wycliffe and the Guild of Nine £5.99
W.J. BURLEY
0-7528-4384-2

☐ Wycliffe and the Beales £5.99
W.J. BURLEY
0-7528-5872-6

☐ Wycliffe and the Winsor Blue £5.99
W.J. BURLEY
0-7528-5873-4

☐ Wycliffe and Death in a Salubrious Place £5.99
W.J. BURLEY
0-7528-6535-8

☐ Wycliffe and the Four Jacks £5.99
W.J. BURLEY
0-7528-4970-0

☐ Wycliffe and the Dead Flautist £5.99
W.J. BURLEY
0-7528-6490-4

☐ Wycliffe's Wild-Goose Chase £5.99
W.J. BURLEY
0-7528-6491-2

☐ Wycliffe and How to Kill a Cat £5.99
W.J. BURLEY
0-7528-8082-9

☐ Wycliffe and the Guilt Edged Alibi £5.99
W.J. BURLEY
0-7528-8083-7

All Orion/Phoenix titles are available at your local bookshop or from the following address:

Mail Order Department
Littlehampton Book Services
FREEPOST BR535
Worthing, West Sussex, BN13 3BR
telephone 01903 828503, *facsimile* 01903 828802
e-mail MailOrders@lbsltd.co.uk
(Please ensure that you include full postal address details)

Payment can be made either by credit/debit card (Visa, Mastercard, Access and Switch accepted) or by sending a £ Sterling cheque or postal order made payable to *Littlehampton Book Services*.

DO NOT SEND CASH OR CURRENCY

Please add the following to cover postage and packing

UK and BFPO:
£1.50 for the first book, and 50p for each additional book to a maximum of £3.50

Overseas and Eire:
£2.50 for the first book plus £1.00 for the second book and 50p for each additional book ordered

---

BLOCK CAPITALS PLEASE

name of cardholder ....

address of cardholder ....

....

....

....

postcode ....

delivery address (if different from cardholder)

....

....

....

....

postcode ....

☐ I enclose my remittance for £..............................

☐ please debit my Mastercard/Visa/Access/Switch (delete as appropriate)

card number ☐☐☐☐☐☐☐☐☐☐☐☐☐☐☐☐

expiry date ☐☐☐☐ Switch issue no. ☐☐

signature ....

prices and availability are subject to change without notice